"The reports said  and it went into his hea

"Yes! I was in shock. He gasped, let go of the and fell. I tried to stop the bleeding, and called 911 right away, but I didn't know what to do. I think he was already dead."

"He was already dead when the paramedics arrived. Why did you leave the knife in?"

"Because I'd seen on TV that taking it out just makes it worse. It all happened so fast."

"How many times did he hit you?"

"Too many to count. I'm trying to write you a history of our relationship. It's so hard to keep it all straight."

"You never called the police on him?"

Claire hung her head, not meeting her eyes. "I know what you're thinking, 'Why didn't I leave?' I didn't think I deserved it, but I did love him and didn't know what to do. Sometimes things were idyllic. It was like living with Dr. Jekyll and Mr. Hyde. Plus, he was an OU football legend, and his family has all the money in the world. I was nobody. Who would've believed me? He told me that all the time. He would end me if I told or left him. He would just casually talk about how easy it would be for me to disappear in the woods."

Sooner Secrets

by

Shelley L. Levisay

Sooner Secrets

Cover Art by *Tina Lynn Stout*

The Wild Rose Press, Inc.
PO Box 708
Adams Basin, NY 14410-0708
Visit us at www.thewildrosepress.com

Publishing History
First Edition, 2022
Trade Paperback ISBN 978-1-5092-3791-3
Digital ISBN 978-1-5092-3792-0

Published in the United States of America

Dedication

To my friends David McKenzie, Kent Bridge, Karen Byars, Cregg Webb, David Hammer, and many others who have spent years working as public defenders.

Chapter 1

Ashley bolted up in bed when she heard her momma's shrieks.

"Aww. No, Devon, please. Not again. I'm sorry."

Ashley slowly slid out of bed and walked on her tiptoes from her room and sneaked parallel against the wall to a hidden nook under an end table. She sat down just in time to watch her daddy drag her momma by the hair from their room to the kitchen. She moved farther back to avoid detection.

"You're just worthless," her daddy yelled. "You had one job tonight. One. And you couldn't even do that right." He released her momma, grabbed something from the fridge, and set it on the counter. "Do you call this dinner? It looks like slop. You knew these were important clients of mine, and you embarrass me by serving them this?"

Her heart raced, and she tried not to make a sound. She knew that if her daddy caught her, her momma would be in more trouble. She felt helpless. *How can my daddy who takes me for ice cream and buys me dolls all the time be so mean to Momma? I don't know what to do. I love Mommy and Daddy. Why do they have to fight?*

"They loved it. What's wrong with it?"

"It might have been fine in the trailer park you grew up in, but not for my clients. They were being polite. We've been married for years, and you're still that backwoods hick. I think you wanted to embarrass me."

"I didn't. I'm sorry. You should've told me what you wanted."

She heard the jarring sound of flesh on flesh before her momma's cry. She shivered, and goosebumps covered her arms.

"Don't talk back to me! You're trying to blame me for your own failures. You won't make that mistake again."

She peered around the corner and saw her parents playing a cat-and-mouse game as her momma tried to run away, but he was like a cat ready to pounce. Momma bolted around the kitchen island but didn't get far before Daddy tackled her to the ground. She couldn't help the "Ah" that came out of her mouth. She peed her pants a little, terrified that Daddy might have heard her, but the sound of them hitting the tile floor echoed throughout the house.

The eerie silence that followed filled the air for what seemed like an eternity. She thought she might throw up when she heard her daddy whisper, "I see you want to play. Well, you know the punishment for running away."

Daddy scooped her momma up in what looked like a wrestling move and slammed her against the counter. As Momma bounced off the counter, he turned her around and began squeezing her neck.

She moved into the room and saw her momma's arms flailing and struggling against him. She wanted to save her momma, but what could she do?

Then, her daddy fell to the ground with a knife in

his back, blood pooling underneath him. She stood staring in a trance, until her momma saw her and screamed, "Ashley! It'll be ok. I promise, but listen to me, go back to bed. You don't know anything. Don't talk to anyone about this! Do you hear me? Just forget it."

"But, but Momma?"

"Not now! Get back in bed!"

****

But as she sat in the fetal position on the creaky and uncomfortable wooden bench, she couldn't forget it. Her momma's terrifying cries echoed in her mind, and she replayed her daddy falling to the ground over and over. This lady who took her to a strange place where she had to share a room with three other girls kept trying to talk to her, but she ignored her, until the woman dragged her inside the courtroom.

Inside, another lady tried to talk to her. Then, a woman in a long black robe rushed in. As Ashley looked around, she saw her Nana Lara with a guy dressed like a gangster. Her eyes widened as she saw her mom on the other side of the room in handcuffs and an oversized orange jumpsuit. It didn't even look like her momma.

The lady in the black robe started asking questions, and the gangster guy started talking about them. She was confused about what was happening, but she saw her momma crying and sinking to the floor. When she realized her mom was leaving, she screamed and ran toward her. "Momma! Momma!" But before she could reach her momma, her nana stalked toward her, glared at her, and declared, "Ashley, honey, you're going home with me. You can't see her now."

She howled, fought to get away from her nana, and ran after her mom around the corner. Her momma shouted, "I love you, baby girl," before she disappeared.

Her nana was already at her side again, and she saw the same look her daddy always had when he was mad and trying to hide it. "Come on, Ashley, let's go eat pancakes, and then we can get you settled into your room at my house," Nana coaxed and squeezed her hand so hard she couldn't squirm away.

Once they were alone in the car, Nana said, "Ashley, now if you're a good girl, eat your pancakes, and don't give me any trouble, you can go pick out a puppy at the shelter, but if you give me trouble, you won't like it."

She just nodded. She'd never liked her nana because she was always mean to her mom. Nana called a bunch of friends and bragged about getting custody of her. "You should have seen that little gold digger Claire in the orange jumpsuit. I'll make sure she rots in there!" Tears silently streamed down her face.

Chapter 2

Jenna Miller sat in the courtroom waiting for her new murder client's arraignment to come on the monitor for her video arraignment. Judge Koepke called Claire Brown's name and pronounced, "Ms. Brown, you have been charged with Murder in the First Degree. You have been appointed an attorney, Ms. Miller, who is in the courtroom today. Right now, I am setting your bond at one million dollars. Your attorney, I'm sure, will be making an argument on that, but I don't have time to hear that today. Ms. Miller, anything you would like me to relay to your client?"

"Yes, Ms. Brown, I'm sure you have questions, but please do not speak to anyone but me about this case."

"Ms. Brown, did you hear the good advice from your attorney?"

"Yes, ma'am."

"Ok, see you in two weeks."

Jenna looked at the terrified woman. At least she was smart enough not to argue with the judge or ask stupid questions.

While waiting for the rest of the jail appearances to finish, she noticed that the motion she brought to file had a mistake on it. *Dang it! Why can't I get these things done right?* Her breath quickened, and her heart raced. She had at least three other court appearances and motions to draft still today, and her patience was thin. Her client, Jeffery Thomas, touched her on the arm.

She recoiled. "What?"

"How do you think the hearing is going? I mean, I did signal. That cop is lying because he's been trying to catch me."

"Jeff, I told you arguing the cop is lying does nothing at this hearing. This is a preliminary hearing. Just trust me to do my job."

"Do you think they will come off of the twenty years, then?"

"It is not time to talk about that. Let me work on getting the charges dismissed. Let's finish this hearing first, and next time don't drive around with a pound of meth in your car."

"I know, I know."

When Judge Koepke finished the video arraignments, she turned back to the courtroom. "Back on the record in the State v. Jeffery Thomas. Ms. Miller, you may now cross-examine Officer Gibson."

Jenna strode to the podium. "Officer Gibson, you testified that you initiated a traffic stop for failure to signal, correct?"

"Yes, that is why I pulled him over."

"Did you write him a ticket for that offense?"

The officer mumbled, "No."

"Why not?"

"Because the stop took another turn."

"But after you took his driver's license and insurance and ran those you came back to the car, correct?"

"Yes."

"Why?"

"To give his information back. I was going to let him off with a warning, but I saw a glass pipe and decided to run the drug dog around."

"A marijuana pipe, right?"

"Yes, it was."

"Were you aware that he had a medical marijuana card?"

"No, I wasn't."

"Did you bother to ask him?"

"No, I didn't feel I needed to because this certainly gave me cause to run my dog around the vehicle, since that is not a search."

"Sir, as a part of your training you are made aware of current search and seizure laws, correct?"

"I'm not a lawyer, but yes, I take continuing education courses."

"So, then you are aware of the recent Supreme Court case that explains you can't extend a traffic stop for a dog sniff?"

"Yes, and I didn't without cause."

"No further questions."

"State, any redirect?" Judge Koepke asked.

"No, Your Honor, and the State rests," the prosecutor replied.

"Defendant?"

"Your Honor, I would demur because of a bad search. Gibson just admitted that he only called the dog out after he had decided to send him on with a warning—the exact thing Rodriguez forbid."

"Ms. Miller, what about seeing the pipe? Would that not give him reason to continue the stop?"

"No, Your Honor, it was a marijuana pipe, which he could legally possess in Oklahoma with a medical

7

card. He didn't ask any questions or anything before getting the dog."

"State, your response?"

Jeremy Hall, a recent law grad, rose and stammered, "Officer Gibson said that he saw a glass pipe. That gives him reasonable suspicion to extend the stop."

"Mr. Hall, if someone has a medical marijuana card, is it a crime to have a pipe?"

"No, Your Honor, but the officer doesn't have to assume that a person has a card."

"But wouldn't it be the officer's duty to inquire further rather than just resorting to a dog sniff to extend the stop?"

"I'm not sure he had that duty, but if he did, he acted in good faith on seeing that glass pipe."

"I am finding the search was unlawful and, therefore, dismissing the case. Mr. Thomas, you are free to go."

"Aw, Jenna, you are the best! Thank you." Jeff put his arm around her, and her body immediately stiffened up.

"You're welcome, but try to stay out of trouble." She sidestepped out of his reach and headed back to her office to fix the motion, wash her hands, and take a lint roller to her outfit.

Chapter 3

Jenna's shoes clicked across the linoleum floor as she walked into the sterile chemotherapy room. "Hey, Auntie. How's it going in here today?"

Aunt Rose, who raised Jenna since her parents died in a car accident when she was two, was battling stage two breast cancer. She lay there covered in blankets chewing ice chips. "I'm tired, but hanging in. How was court today?"

"I got my client's case dismissed this morning, so a pretty good day."

Rose yawned and gave her a thumbs up before falling asleep.

Jenna settled into the chair beside her aunt and read a book while waiting for her IV to finish. The smell of antiseptic permeated the air. She looked at the other patients fighting their own battles with cancer. All different ages and backgrounds, but all fighting the same battle. *Cancer doesn't discriminate.*

The nurse came in a half hour later cheering. "Another one down, Rose. Only two more to go!"

"I know! No offense, but I hope to never come back here again!"

"None taken, but maybe we will run into each other at Wal-Mart. Don't forget bland food for the next day or so. Do you need any more nausea meds?"

"We still have a few left from last time. Half of one

9

pill knocks Aunt Rose out for several hours."

"Take care of her."

"I will."

When they arrived at Aunt Rose's home, two large Maine Coon cats greeted them at the door. Jenna settled Rose into bed and fed the cats. She preferred the company of cats to people.

After watching Rose sleep for a while, she headed home and thought back to before her world fell apart: back when she had a social life and she still had the love of her life, Erik.

She was a musical theater major who loved singing and performing. Back then, she was carefree and innocent. Erik was a gifted tenor, and the two performed gigs together almost every weekend and were in several musical theater productions together. They planned to make their living by opening a music studio and performing any chance they could. They knew they would scrape by but would be doing what they loved.

But all those plans came to a screeching halt when Erik went to jail. A swarm of police surrounded Erik's house and ordered him to surrender. He barricaded himself and refused to leave. She tried to get him to surrender over the police radio, but he kept raging about things that didn't make any sense. SWAT threw tear gas in his house that knocked him out before dragging him out in cuffs.

She hadn't known what happened to her sweet and talented fiancé, but she went to every court appearance and visited him in jail, but he blamed her for his arrest.

His anger and rejection shattered her, and ten years later, her heart was still broken. Her guilt over the shooting led her to attend law school to become a defense lawyer and help others struggling with mental illness and drug addiction.

As she walked in her condo, her black cat jumped on her shoulder nearly knocking her off balance. She rescued Midnight when she was only four weeks old. The now four-year-old cat cared only for Jenna and had a supernatural ability to disappear when others entered the place.

"Midnight, geez, I'm happy to see you too, but a little space would be nice."

She relaxed on the couch, ordered dinner in, and turned on the television to hear, "From the courthouse today, the district attorney charged Claire Brown with murdering her husband, Devon Brown, who most people remember as a former linebacker for the OU Sooners' last national championship team. The probable cause affidavit says that Mrs. Brown stabbed her husband in the back. We will keep you advised as we know more."

Great, I haven't even gotten to read the discovery yet or talk to her and they are already poisoning my potential jurors.

She tried to put the events of the day to bed by playing her new phone game obsession Best Fiends until the jail calls rang back-to-back to back.

"Ah!! Take the hint, I don't want to take your phone calls right now!" She ranted aloud at the phone.

She always had work to do, but she needed a break tonight. Sensing her frustration, Midnight walked back and forth across her lap and demanded attention.

Chapter 4

Claire had two cellmates. First, Traunya, an imposing six-foot-tall woman, in for drug distribution this time with her beau, the biggest meth dealer in town. The other was Candice, a junkie who weighed eighty-five pounds, charged with forging checks. She shook her head and wondered how she ended up here. *I can't stand this place or these people. I don't deserve to be in here. Devon was not who they thought he was.* She thought back to when she met him.

Fall 2009

She was a freshman attending a sorority party at the University of Oklahoma when the best-looking man she'd ever seen approached her. "Hey, princess, why aren't you dancing?"

"I'm waiting for a good song to come on."

"What do you want to hear? I have an in with the DJ, and he'll play anything to help me get a dance."

"I don't recall agreeing to dance with you. I don't even know your name."

"Sorry, doll, I'm Devon. I haven't asked you to dance yet, but you will be dancing with me." He leaned in close, his lips almost touching her cheek. "Come on, tell me a song you want to hear."

She paused for a second, nervous and excited that this guy was so close to her, before croaking, " 'Makes Me Wonder' by Maroon 5."

"You got it." He walked into the crowd to find the DJ.

The first strains of "Makes Me Wonder" started to play as soon as the current song ended. A smile slowly came to her lips as he appeared in front of her with his hand out, his eyebrow raised, and his eyes penetrating her soul. "Can I get your name now?"

"Claire." He pulled her to him and walked with his arm around her to the dance floor. They danced to that and then to Kid Rock's "All Summer Long," David Archuleta's "Crush," and many other hits. It was like the two of them were the only ones present at that party as they danced the night away. After a couple hours, he suggested they get out of there and get a drink or something. She went along without a second thought, forgetting about the girlfriends she came with.

Devon wasn't like any of the other guys she'd been around. He exuded confidence and an indefinable quality that made her weak in the knees just by his presence. He walked her to his Mustang convertible and drove her to a small college bar near the campus that wasn't too crowded

They sat and talked about anything and everything. She was from a small town in Oklahoma and had only dated her high school sweetheart. His family lived in Nichols Hills, and he grew up in luxury, and his status as a football player for the Sooners elevated his popularity on campus. His entire attention was focused on her despite the bartender flirting with him from the moment they walked in. She felt special because he focused all his attention on her—a naive freshman who'd barely been on campus for a month.

He drove her back to her dorm and walked her up

to the front doors and cupped her face. "I would kiss you, but this wasn't an official date. I'll wait until then."

Heart racing, she glanced down. "Are we going on a date?"

He pulled her face up to look at him. "Yep, tomorrow night, I'll pick you up and we'll go for a fancy dinner somewhere and then to the movies, but you better come watch me play first."

"I already planned on going to the game, but I have to admit I don't know much about football."

"That's refreshing, so many girls are just falling all over me because I'm a football player, but you're special," he whispered as he leaned down and gingerly kissed her on the forehead.

****

In the window seat on the second floor of the Victorian house, Ashley played with Zeus, her new miniature cocker spaniel. *He's the only good thing about living here.*

Nana yelled from the downstairs foyer, "Ashley, you need to get dressed in the new dress I got you so we can go to the club party!"

She puffed out her lip. "I don't wanna go. I don't like the kids at the club."

"You will do as you're told. I won't hear another word about it."

"Can Zeus come?"

"No, now go get dressed."

A few minutes later, they left for the Easter party. "Ashley, I used to take your father to all of these same parties at the club. I'll show you pictures when we get back home. There will be an Easter egg contest. You'll like that."

I wish she would just leave me alone. I miss Momma.

When they arrived at the club, the Easter bunny took pictures with her and all the other kids. Then, the Easter egg hunt started after a whistle. They started the hunt, and she picked up several eggs when she heard Nana talking with another woman. "Doesn't Ashley look just like Devon?"

"Yes, she's beautiful. At least you have a little piece of Devon in her."

"Hopefully, that mother of hers gets convicted soon and then I can adopt her and keep her forever."

Forever? Oh no!

"You'll get in trouble for listening in," another girl whispered to Ashley.

She jumped back. "What?"

"I've gotten spanked for listening to adult conversations. My name's Lizzie."

"Well, I'm not going to get caught."

"Come over this way and you can hear more and not be seen."

She followed her behind the bushes. "I'm Ashley."

"I know. We all know who you are. Did your mom really kill your dad?"

Ashley looked down. "I can't talk about that, but you don't know what it was like. Daddy was mean to Momma."

"So is my stepmom. That's who your grandma is talking to. We better go back with the other kids before they come looking for us."

Lara called them over. "Oh, good, it looks like you made a friend! How are you, Miss Lizzie? You look

15

lovely today."

"Thanks, Mrs. Brown."

Lizzie's stepmom spoke up then. "Lara, since they have become friends, why doesn't Ashley come for a play date tomorrow?"

Lara beamed. "That sounds lovely. How about we come over about four?"

"Wonderful."

Chapter 5

Jenna marched into the courtroom for the preliminary hearing conference docket, displaying more confidence than she felt. At this docket, she would receive a plea offer and police reports from the prosecutors, which was all they had to provide.

She walked over to Claire sitting in cuffs with the other inmates surrounding the room. "Hey, I'm Jenna, we saw each other on video previously. I'm going to set your case for the quickest preliminary hearing we can get."

"What's that?"

"It's a probable cause hearing. You are facing life in prison because of the first-degree murder charge. I want to see the witnesses on the stand."

"Aren't you going to ask me my side of things? Don't we need to talk about everything?"

"Not now, and certainly not in this courtroom where other people can overhear you. I don't need or want to know your side until I have read all of the discovery, but I will visit you in jail before the next court date."

"Look, I have a daughter out there, and this is my life. Are you going to fight for me or not? This wasn't my fault. He was attacking me."

She clicked her pen back and took a deep breath. "I'm here to ensure that the State can prove their case against you beyond a reasonable doubt and protect your Constitutional rights. I can't worry about your daughter and sounds like you weren't thinking about her when this happened."

"Miss, I know you don't know me, but don't ever talk about my daughter again. She is everything to me. You don't understand, and that's what I'm trying to tell you. I don't care about me, but I do care about getting back to my daughter and keeping her from being raised by the same bitch that raised my late husband."

She felt for this woman, but her feelings had gotten her into trouble before. She had to keep that professional distance.

"Claire, my job is to zealously defend you and to protect your rights. I get that you are scared and frustrated. I've been doing this for seven years and am successful. Just because I'm not holding your hand doesn't mean I'm not doing my job. I'm here to make sure the government doesn't railroad you. I'm not here to be your friend."

"Ok. How long until I can get out?"

"This process is going to be long and painful, so you need to settle in for the long haul. Now, I have nine other clients who are also locked up and need my attention, but let me be clear, you and I will talk about everything at the right time."

She moved on to her next client who picked up his third larceny in a year. "Don, the State wants ten years in prison. I can't really tell how they can connect you to this theft, so let's set this for hearing and see what they have."

"I'll take drug court."

"Right now, they aren't offering that, but I will

work on them."

"What about a bond reduction?"

"I'll ask, but probably not going to happen, and you likely lose me if you bond out."

"You know that's not fair."

"Unfortunately, that's the way our system works. Court system just doesn't have enough money to supply court appointed counsel for people that bond out of jail. Give me a little time."

She worked her way down the line with a couple burglaries and stolen vehicles and drug deals. She'd been doing this for seven years and now could review these probable cause affidavits quickly and break it down for the clients just as fast.

Jerrod, one of her repeat offenders, exclaimed, "Look, Jenna, you've done me solid before. I get I may have to do time, but that search was whack. You gonna file one of those motions you do?"

"You're still on probation from your last case, so it's not going to be all that simple because they only have to prove that it is more likely than not that you violated your probation with this arrest. Once the State shows that, the Judge can and will throw you in prison whether or not the DA can prove you are guilty beyond a reasonable doubt on this new case."

Two assistant district attorneys were at the docket today: Mary Ann and Blake. Mary Ann was an uptight, conservative, but talented frenemy. Blake was about her age but went to a different law school. Because of the shared experience of law school and the bar exam, many attorneys working in the same practice area become fast acquaintances at least. Not in this case. She hated Mary Ann and Blake, but the feel was mutual.

"Jenna, why are you setting all these prelims? Let's just get these pled out. You know these people are guilty," Blake complained.

"If you say they're guilty, case closed, let's just hang them now. Sorry I'm going to make you do your job."

Mary Ann interjected. "You don't think they are actually innocent, do you? You've been doing this long enough to know better."

"Doesn't matter what I think. They still have Constitutional rights, or have you forgotten that?"

"You can forget about any deal on Claire Brown. She stabbed her husband in the back with her daughter sleeping a few feet away."

She gathered up her files and looked over at a terrified Claire, who didn't fit in there, but her clients had fooled her before. In her first year of practice, she poured her heart into fighting for this twenty-year-old guy charged with domestic assault and battery. He was so slick and smooth that she believed him when he said that the whole thing was a misunderstanding and blown out of proportion. She took the case to trial, and the jury returned a not guilty verdict.

It was a year later when she saw him in orange coveralls again, but this time, he was charged with domestic abuse on a pregnant woman and for causing her miscarriage. When she questioned him, he coolly told her that his girlfriend got an attitude and he had to subdue her. It wasn't his fault that she lost the baby. He was a sociopath without any remorse.

She questioned her own judgment from then on. First, she didn't realize her fiancé was crazy, and he shot an innocent man Then, she believed and helped free a sociopath who killed a baby.

A year later, she helped a meth and pain pill addict named Paula. She gave her a chance to work for her and gain self-confidence by letting her be her personal assistant, and what did the addict do? Paula stole several checks from her and took several pieces of jewelry to feed her habit. She even paid a deposit and first month's rent and utilities for Paula and her daughter. She even became close to Paula's teenage daughter, but they played a long con on her. After that she decided it was best just not to care and not get close to anyone.

What if Claire was right? How can I represent her well if I assume that she's guilty too? She took Claire's file home with her that night.

Chapter 6

Claire was more depressed than ever on the ride back to the jail. That lawyer seemed smart, but eccentric and bossy. *Two more months! I hope Ashley is okay. Will we even have a place when I get out?*

She continued writing in the journal of her life with Devon for Jenna.

Spring 2010

Devon was so attentive. He showered her with gifts and compliments. He walked her to class anytime his schedule allowed. She spent all her free time with him. If she made plans with her sorority sisters, he insisted on coming along or her staying with him instead. She was eighteen and didn't know any better. He was her first love. She was the envy of most girls on campus. Everyone treated him like a god around campus.

She was apprehensive the first time he took her to meet his parents. She was so nervous that they wouldn't think she was good enough for him because she grew up with her mom and baby sister in a double-wide trailer, while they lived in this mansion in Nichols Hills. Lara was every bit the nightmare she feared and worse.

That first day as soon as the two of them were alone, Lara warned, "If you don't make him happy, I will end you. You will sign a pre-nup if this relationship gets that far. I'm not going to let a gold-

22

digging tramp take our family money when it doesn't work out. You are not in our class. I'm not even sure I could make you over enough to at least fake it."

She swore she would win her over and worked to be the perfect girlfriend. He proposed at the spring fling after seven months of dating and scheduled a wedding date for that summer since he was graduating. It was a whirlwind romance. He treated her like a princess, and she thought he was Prince Charming. The jealousy and possessiveness he displayed were just signs of how much he loved her. At least that's what she thought until the honeymoon when she laughed at another man's joke. The look he gave her chilled her to the bone.

When they walked back to their hotel room that night, he pinned her to the wall and hissed, "You're my wife. You don't flagrantly flirt with other men ever, do you understand?"

She shivered. "I'm sorry. I didn't mean anything by it. You know I only love you."

He released her, and his voice returned to normal. "Don't do it again, ok, sweetheart? It's embarrassing and disrespectful."

She nodded, her mind reeling. The next morning, he brought her flowers, a tennis bracelet, and ordered elaborate room service. Neither mentioned it again. The rest of the honeymoon was idyllic on the Hawaiian beach, but little did she know that would set a precedent for her future.

Present

She had to do something besides just sit in her jail cell to find out about Ashley. Since her marriage to Devon, her relationship with her family deteriorated.

She had no friends of her own anymore—only their couple friends, and she didn't think any of the women would help her. While she thought the distance between her and her mom was insurmountable, she had no one else. She knew that her mom loved her and certainly wouldn't hold her actions against her daughter. She just hoped her mom hadn't given up on her.

"Dear Mom, I know it's been too long, and I'm sure you're disappointed in me, but don't believe the news. I'm sorry that I let Devon come between us, but I didn't know what to do. Devon always told me that the only way I would ever leave him would be in a casket. If I had managed to leave, he would never let me take Ashley, and I couldn't risk that. You know how much money his family has and how beloved he was, and I just knew they would find a way to win in court and keep her from me. I don't know if I will get out of this, but you must fight for Ashley. You can't let Lara ruin her life too. I love you!"

"Ginger, what are you doing just crying and writing in here all day?" Traunya quizzed.

She ignored her question. "Hey, do you think you're better than me or something?" Traunya snapped.

This kind of questioning went on all the time, and she finally had enough. "Look, you don't know anything about me. I've been through hell the last few years, so just leave me alone!"

"Oh, girl, you have fire in you. All right, come on out with the rest of us. You can't survive here all alone. Better make friends since you will be here awhile."

She nodded and followed her into the dayroom, realizing that Traunya was right.

Sooner Secrets

Chapter 7

The metal detector sounded as Jenna walked into the jail hoping to see Claire. "I'm going to have to look into your bag, ma'am," the detention officer said.

"That's fine. My keys are in there, but I left my phone in the car."

The guard walked her into the attorney interview room, and she waited another fifteen minutes for her client to arrive. She scribbled notes on her legal pad because it seemed like forever without her iPhone or iPad. Claire finally arrived—her eyes puffy and dark. The guard cuffed one arm to the bench and left one arm free.

"Hey, Claire, how are you doing today?"

"This place is terrible, and every day without my daughter is killing me, but I'm hanging in best I can."

"I've read the police reports and listened to the 911 call. You sound distraught but also don't give any clue that someone else stabbed your husband. You gave no statement to the police, which was smart, but only you, your late husband, and your daughter were in the home, so it doesn't really leave much room for a defense. So, what happened?"

"Where to start? That night we had company over—one of his clients and his wife and another colleague and his wife. His client complimented my food, and I don't know if that made him jealous or what, but once they left, he just lost it. He dragged me by the hair and complained that I made trailer trash food and embarrassed him. He backhanded me, tackled me, and strangled me. I remember not being able to breathe and worrying that I would die. I just reached and grabbed for anything to hit him and get him off me."

"The reports said that he was stabbed in the back, and it went into his heart. Did you try to help him?"

"Yes! I was just in shock. I remember he gasped and let go of me and just kind of fell. I tried to stop the bleeding, and I immediately called 911, but I didn't know what to do. I think he was already dead."

"He was already dead when the paramedics arrived. Why did you leave the knife in?"

"Because I'd seen on TV that taking it out just makes it worse. It all happened so fast."

"How many times did he hit you?"

"Too many to count. I'm trying to write you a history of our relationship. It's so hard to keep it all straight."

"You never called the police on him?"

Claire hung her head, not meeting her eyes. "I know what you're thinking, 'Why didn't I leave?' I didn't think I deserved it, but I did love him and didn't know what to do. Sometimes things were idyllic. It was like living with Dr. Jekyll and Mr. Hyde. Plus, he was an OU football legend, and his family has all the money in the world. I was nobody. Who would have believed me? He told me that all the time. He would end me if I told or left him. He would just casually talk about how easy it would be for me to disappear in the woods."

"Unfortunately, that is pretty typical. Were you on

the bank accounts?"

"No, he only gave me an allowance to buy groceries and supplies. All credit cards were in his name, and he always monitored their use. His phone alerted him every time I used one."

"What about when you had a child?"

"He would have taken her away from me; she was my reason for living! I would have endured anything to be with her."

Of course, she would have stayed once she was pregnant. She clicked her pen trying to block out the images of that pregnant young woman and the baby she lost.

"Did he ever hurt Ashley?"

She shook her head. "No. She was his little princess. He never hurt her. I was the one who disappointed him."

"I know she's young, but she had to know what was going on."

She slammed her palm on the table. "Look, I kept it away from her the best I could. She had everything she ever wanted. She lived in a beautiful house in a nice neighborhood. She went to private school. I wasn't going to take her from all of that to move to a women's shelter or something," Claire hissed.

"I'm not trying to upset you, but you need to understand the State is going to come at you for this a lot harder than I am. Where was your daughter that night?"

"She was asleep. She doesn't know anything, but she's with my mother-in-law, who is the reason Devon was the way he was. She knew how he was and would scold me for not being supportive enough of him."

"Ever seek medical treatment for your injuries?"

Claire buried her face in her hands. "I had to go to the ER a couple of times, but I always lied about what happened. If I didn't promise to tell his story, he wouldn't take me. One doctor didn't believe me because he kept asking me and finding excuses for Devon to leave."

"This isn't your fault, Claire. Will you sign this medical release?"

"Whatever you need, but are you going to fight for me?"

"I know I'm tough, but that's who you want in the courtroom. I'm going to get an investigator to research Devon's past and see if we can find any proof of his being violent with anyone else. If it is just your word after he is dead, it will be hard, but we will give it our all. I'm also going to have a domestic violence expert visit you. Please cooperate with her. She could be our best ally.

"Did you ever tell anyone?"

"I hinted at it with my mom and sister, but I didn't see them much. I wrote to my mom the other day. I'm praying she will write back. Devon made himself my world. He didn't want me to work, so I didn't really see anyone except his mother and her friends at the club or volunteering. Those women saw me with bruises, scratches, and other injuries, but I always stuck to the agreed cover stories."

"What about your neighbors? Would they have overheard arguments or seen anything?"

"Possibly, but that neighborhood minds their own business."

"Like I said, I'll send an investigator and an expert

out and see what else we can find to support our defense. I'll see you at prelim. Keep your head up!"

Chapter 8

When Jenna arrived at her office, a tall man in a leather jacket was standing inside her lobby reading a picture. Her heart stopped when he turned around. If she didn't know better, she would swear that he was Zac Efron. She shot a puzzled look at her assistant, who knew she didn't like unscheduled appointments, especially first thing in the morning. Then the man stepped forward. "I'm Jaxson Stone, the investigator you requested. I came to get a copy of the file to get started."

Normally, the investigators the public defender's office hired were retired policemen, who were a lot older and gruffer than him. She stuttered, "Come on in."

He followed her into the room and made himself comfortable in the chair across from her desk. "Anything in particular that you are hoping I will find?"

"I'd like to find any evidence backing up Claire's story about Devon's abuse. See if anyone knows about Devon's temper, an ex-girlfriend, neighbor, family, or friends. She wants to go to trial as soon as possible because she's in jail and she hasn't gotten to see her daughter since she was locked up."

"Ok, you know this guy was an OU national championship linebacker, right?"

"So? That means he can't be an abuser. Haven't

you watched the news or followed the #metoo movement?" *Ok he may be hot, but he's a jerk.*

"Woah, killer chill out. I'm just telling you that people are going to like him around here. Can I get a copy of the file?"

"Yeah sure, just a second. I didn't know you were coming, or I would have had it ready for you."

"You're one of those Type A, everything has to be scheduled types, aren't you?" She tapped her fingers on her leg, hoping he would leave.

"Yep. That's me. And... I've got a lot of stuff to do today, so I better get after it."

"When's the prelim?"

"Why?"

"Because I'm going to come watch. I like to read people."

"You don't have to do that."

"You want me to do a good investigation, right?"

"Well, yeah, that's a given."

"Then I'm coming to contested hearings. I learn things from them. Sometimes by watching the witnesses that come to those hearings. Just let me do my thing."

"What are your credentials, anyway?"

"I was a police officer and had just made detective when I was shot and had to retire. I've been a private investigator now for about five years. I'll send you an update." He strode out the door without another word.

"Amy, will you find a couple domestic violence experts so I can interview them and get them scheduled with Claire?"

"Sure thing, boss. Here are your files for the misdemeanor docket today."

"Thanks."

****

She settled in at the defense table and called for the first client. "I've read the report. The D.A.'s office indicates that they have spoken to the victim and that he will testify against you. Their offer is a deferred sentence and for you to complete anger management."

"I don't have the money to take that class. That guy started it. I wanna talk to the judge."

"Sir, that's not how this works. You don't get to tell your side until trial. Unless you can post bond, you will remain in jail until that time. Do you want a jury trial or a trial in front of the judge?"

"When will the trial be?"

"The next jury term is in middle May so about six weeks from now. The early bench trial date is about a month away."

"I've got to stay here until then?"

"If you want a trial and can't post a bond, then yes."

"Why can't I just talk to the judge today?"

"Because this is a docket and there is not time, and no one is prepared for a trial today. We don't have witnesses here."

"This isn't right that I gotta sit in jail to try to fight these charges."

"Unfortunately, that is how our system works. What is your bond?"

"Five thousand dollars."

"That's only $500 with a bondsperson. Some will take $250 down and $250 later."

"This is ridiculous. I'll just take the deal so I can go home."

"I can't let you plead guilty unless you admit that you did it, unless they will let you plead no contest."

"Fine, I did it. Let's just get this over with."

After pleading at least thirty people and filling out all that paperwork, she couldn't straighten her fingers out. As she walked to her car, she remembered two things: 1) that she promised Rose she would come by, and 2) that she still needed to write a motion to suppress.

"Rosie, I brought you favorite for dinner."

"Great! I'm back in my room."

"It's like an oven in here. Geez, the thermostat is on 83."

"Jen, I forgot you were coming. I'm so cold. It's been a bad day."

"I'm sorry. I brought your favorite foods. Maybe that will help."

"I'm so nauseated. I can't eat right now."

"You are going to take these pills whether you like it or not. You can at least drink this iced tea. I don't need you dehydrated on top of everything else."

She set up her iPad on the other side of the bed to work on her motion. "What are you doing?"

"I'm going to hang out with you for a while and work on this motion that I need to get done."

"Go home, Jenna! You don't need to babysit me."

"I'm not. I'm spending time with my favorite aunt."

"I'm your only aunt. You need to get a social life, girl. You are too young to just work all the time and take care of an old woman."

"Hush, and you are not that old. Besides, we can enjoy the Seinfeld reruns that should be coming on." A couple hours later, Rose finally ate a little of the Cracker Barrel she brought. After eating, she drifted off to sleep with one cat on the pillow above her head and one at her feet.

Chapter 9

Ashley rang the doorbell, and Lizzie answered almost at once. "Hey, get in here." She followed her in the house as Lizzie led her by the hand up the stairs to her room and slammed the door.

"Look what I've got for you," Lizzie raved as she shows a stamped and addressed envelope.

"What is this?"

"So, I found where your mom is. I took an envelope and stamp from dad's office. So just write to your mom, and we can mail it."

"How did you do that?"

"My iPhone and a little help from my sister. You can find out anything on Google. I can't believe you don't have a phone yet."

"Yeah, I know. Thanks so much. I'm going to write to her and draw her a picture now."

She wrote and drew until her hand hurt. "Lizzie, how are we going to get this to her without anyone knowing?"

"I covered for my big sister when she snuck out the other day, and she still owes me. She'll mail it for us."

"Thanks so much. You're the best friend I've ever had." She rushed over and hugged her.

****

Claire wrote in the journal for Jenna, but she hadn't written anything in several days. Revealing these secrets to someone else was both embarrassing and agonizing.

****

2012

She sat nervously in her doctor's waiting room. Devon insisted she see her doctor because of bad nausea and vomiting. She went to the lab earlier. Nurse came out and called her name, and she headed back into the doctor's office. "Mrs. Brown, I have great news for you. You are six weeks pregnant."

"Oh wow! I can't wait to tell my husband."

She didn't go back to college after they married. She joined the junior service league, volunteered on other committees, and hosted any number of social events that he wanted. She wanted to be a teacher, but he wanted her to stay home. She wanted more in her life, but when she found out she was pregnant, she was over the moon.

Devon unfortunately became more controlling and possessive once she was pregnant. He set up apps on her phone so he could see where she was at all times. He installed cameras both inside and outside their house, but having Ashley made it worth it. From that day on, Ashley was her life. Her driving motiviation to take care of her baby. While she thought the baby would make Devon happy, she walked on eggshells all the time.

Present

"Brown, you've got a visitor," the guard told her and signaled her to exit the cell. She followed him into the family visitor room that was divided by plexiglass. There wasn't a telephone, because you could hear but you couldn't have any physical contact allegedly to

37

keep contraband out, but most of that crooked guards brought in.

She saw her mom sitting on the other side of the glass. Reflexively, her face lit up. "Mom, thank you so much for coming. I love you!"

Her mom, Khara, had tears in her eyes, "Claire, honey, you don't even look like yourself. I just can't believe you're in jail."

"I know, Mom. I should have listened to you and gotten out of there, but I just did what I thought was best at the time."

"No point in rehashing all of that. We have more important things to worry about. I spoke to an attorney about Ashley. We are going to file a motion to have me appointed as her guardian, but he said it was a long shot unless I can show Lara is unfit. Good news is that I should at least be able to get grandparent's visitation."

"That's something."

"Bad news is he also told me that if you are convicted, that could be a reason for Lara to file for adoption, and then I would be battling her to adopt Ashley."

"No! No! No! She cannot have my baby, whatever we need to do. This is all Devon's fault. Lara will screw Ashley up just like she did Devon."

"I know, honey, that's why you have to beat these charges. What can I do to help you?"

"I don't know yet. My attorney won't let me talk to anyone about the case. Her reputation is good."

"Let me know if you don't think she is doing her job. Most of my money is going to the family lawyer, but I could see what we could come up with."

"I don't care about me; just focus on my baby girl."

"In other news, your sister just had a little boy, Justin. He was born seven pounds two ounces."

"Oh wow! Tell her congratulations for me. I have missed so much because of that man." Tears gushed from her eyes. *I wonder if I will get out of her here to ever see my nephew.*

Chapter 10

Jenna walked into the courtroom and saw Jaxson Stone sitting on the back row. He looked nothing like the bad boy she saw last time. He was still hot but looked poised to take over the world. She felt butterflies in her stomach like she hadn't in years. *Great, now I'm self-conscious before I even start this hearing.* She nodded at him but didn't want any spectators to know who he was. While she set up her iPad, her client came in with the jailers. She motioned for Claire to come over.

Mary Ann and Blake came in with their files and victim witness coordinator in tow. "Jenna, this is your last chance to negotiate, if we put on this hearing, no deals."

"Understood, but we have a defense, so I think we'll hear the evidence."

"A defense? You're hanging your hat on a defense? Good luck with that with the evidence we have."

She shook her head and didn't even respond because what was the point?

The Honorable Judge Joseph Murphy came out to start the hearing. He was a young judge, but well-liked by all of those in power, but easy to see why. His charisma showed in his handling of the courtroom. "Are we ready to get this show on the road?"

"State's ready, Your Honor."

"Defense is ready."

"Ok, anything we need to discuss before I hear testimony?"

Mary Ann replied, "No."

She rose. "Judge, we would request that the rule of sequestration be invoked."

"The rule of sequestration has been invoked, so if you are or potentially might be a witness in this case, you need to leave the room. Counsel, police your own witnesses."

Mary Ann signaled to the back, and she saw a woman, whom she assumed to be Lara.

Claire audibly exhaled. "You have no idea how much I can't stand that woman."

"State, call your first witness."

"The State calls Detective Mark Stewart."

The Judge swore him in, and Mary Ann started with the benign introductory questions about his name, employment, and experience. When Mary Ann got to the point, she began taking notes, "Detective Stewart, did you respond to a murder scene at residence in Norman, Oklahoma, on January 21, 2019?"

"Yes, responding officers and paramedics had already arrived and determined that Devon Brown had died presumably from a stab wound."

"When you arrived, what did you see?"

"The coroner arrived at the same time as me, so I saw the deceased lying face down with a knife in his back and blood soaking his shirt."

"Who all was at the scene when you arrived?"

"Responding officers, the coroner, and the deceased's wife and daughter were in the office."

"You said the deceased's wife was there. Did you eventually arrest her?"

"Yes, I did."

"Do you see her in the courtroom today?"

"Yes, she is in an orange jumpsuit at the table next to her attorney, Ms. Miller," Detective Stewart answered.

"Did you send the knife that was in his back to the lab for testing?"

"Yes, we requested fingerprints, DNA, and trace evidence."

"What were the results of that testing?"

"The Defendant's fingerprints were on the knife, and there were also several smudged fingerprints. The deceased's blood was on the knife. We also found a reddish-brown hair on the knife."

"Were you able to match the hair to anyone?"

"No, there was no DNA on the hair."

"What else did you notice about the scene?" the prosecutor asked

"Well mostly that it was in pristine condition other than the dead body."

"Did it appear that any kind of struggle had taken place?"

"Not at all."

"Did you interview the Defendant?" Mary Ann asked.

"I tried. The Defendant was almost inconsolable, so before I took her down to the station, I let her say goodbye to her daughter. I left her in the room alone for about an hour. When I came back in, I asked her what happened. The only thing she said was, 'This wasn't supposed to happen.' "

"No further questions, Your Honor."

"Cross?" The Judge asked looking at her, but it's a foregone conclusion that she will cross this witness.

"Yes, Your Honor." She walked to the podium. "Detective, did you investigate about what happened before the stabbing?"

"No, I didn't see anything that indicated there was a struggle in the home."

"Did you talk to the daughter?"

"No, we have forensic interviewers that conduct those type interviews. Child welfare would have set that up if they thought she witnessed anything," the detective answered.

"You didn't interview the only other person at home at the time of the murder?"

"The Defendant said that the child was asleep. I don't want to traumatize children any more than necessary. Her father was dead, and her mother was being arrested."

"I understand perhaps not that night, but wouldn't you think it would be important to talk to the only other person in the home?" she asked with her palms outstretched in a question.

"It was my understanding that she wouldn't talk to anyone about that night."

"Did you even attempt to ask the child about her parents' relationship or investigate her claim that he was attacking her that night?"

The detective raised one eyebrow and smiled tightly. "No, there was no need to do that. All evidence pointed to the Defendant, and she never denied it."

"Objection, move to strike that last comment." Her knuckles tapped on the podium.

"Detective, you know better than that," the Judge admonished.

"So, you mentioned that her fingerprints were on the knife along with several smudged ones, correct?"

"Yes."

"Were Mr. Brown's fingerprints on the knife?"

"I don't know. That's a better question for the fingerprint expert."

"I'm not asking for an expert opinion, but when the prosecutor asked you about evidence, you were able to answer. Were his prints on the knife?"

"I believe so."

"Would you agree that it's normal to find a stay-at-home wife and mom's prints on a knife in their kitchen?"

"I don't know about normal because every situation is different, but not uncommon."

"This reddish-brown hair—you can't link that to anyone in particular, right?"

"No, but it looked the same color as your client's hair." The detective pointed at Claire.

"Even if it were her hair, wouldn't you expect to find a wife's hair on her husband?"

"No, not necessarily."

"To sum up your case, your evidence is that my client and the deceased were the only adults in the home. He's dead; she's not, therefore she must have committed murder, does that about sum it up?" Jenna snarked.

"Objection, argumentative," Mary Ann sniped.

"I'll withdraw the question."

"I want to respond to her question," Detective Stewart piped up.

"It's been withdrawn," Judge Murphy answered. "Move along, Ms. Miller."

"You can't disprove that the deceased attacked my client, can you?" she grilled.

"I found no evidence of any attack."

"Did you or another officer examine my client for any marks or bruises?"

"If I had seen any or she had said anything about an attack, I would have had a female detective do that, but saw no apparent injuries."

"But no exam was performed, correct?"

"No."

"In your experience investigating domestic violence are all injuries visible?"

"I don't know."

"Specifically, can you see bruises on someone's head?"

"Not always."

"What actual investigation did you conduct?"

"What do you mean?"

"Did you interview any other witnesses about their marriage?"

"No, I saw no reason to do any of that. I don't have to show motive, but she did stand to inherit a million-dollar life insurance policy."

She had questions she wanted to ask about the insurance, but it would be a rookie mistake to ask questions when she didn't already know the answers.

"How did you learn about the life insurance policies?"

"From the deceased's mother Lara Brown."

"Did you talk to any members of the Defendant's family?"

"No, and I didn't go out of my way to talk to Mrs. Brown. She came to see me."

"So, you only got the deceased family's version?"

"I did my job."

"Nothing further, Your Honor."

"Any redirect?"

"No, Judge."

"Sir, you are free to go," the judge said to the witness and turned back to the State. "Any further witnesses?"

"No, Your Honor, but I would offer State's Exhibit 1 which is the Medical Examiner's report which is allowed at preliminary hearing without the witness."

"Counsel, any objection?"

"Not for purposes of this hearing."

"State's Exhibit 1 is admitted without objection. Anything further?"

"With that the State rests and asks that the Court bind over the Defendant on the charge of Murder in the First Degree and the alternative count of Murder in the Second Degree." Mary Ann smirked at her.

"Ms. Miller?" The judge looked for a response.

"Your Honor, I would demur to the evidence particularly on the element of premeditation for Murder in the First Degree. The State did not put on any direct evidence except a fingerprint on the weapon that was in her own house tying my client to the murder. All evidence was circumstantial. My client did not admit to the murder. What the State is calling an admission is not an admission at all. Certainly, even if circumstantial evidence were sufficient to show this low burden of murder, but not on premeditation."

The judge looked to Mary Ann, and she was

already on her feet. "Judge, we asked for alternative counts, but have every reason to believe that we can prove First Degree Murder with premeditation because as the Court knows, premeditation can be proven in a second. Contained within the Medical Examiner's report are descriptions of the fatal wound, and the knife went all the way in without hesitation. Again, the burden is only probable cause for this preliminary hearing, and we have met that burden."

The judge ruled. "For purposes of this hearing, I find probable cause for Murder in the First Degree and the alternative count of Murder in the Second Degree. As counsel for the Defendant is aware, many of her arguments may be excellent for closing arguments at trial, but this is only a preliminary hearing, and the State showed threshold requirement of probable cause. When would you like your arraignment?"

"My client would waive thirty days for arraignment. I would like the 31st day of July at 9:00 A.M."

"No, I don't waive my thirty days. I want the quickest day available!" Claire interrupted.

"I'll give you a moment to discuss with your client," Judge Murphy said.

"Claire, don't ever interrupt me in court again. We need time to finish our investigation and have the expert ready. Trust me on this."

"While I'm rotting in here and my daughter is living with that woman!"

"You only get one shot at this. If a jury finds you guilty, you will be in prison for life and will never see your daughter outside of a prison cell. So, you need to give me time. The earliest we can get to a jury trial is

47

September anyway because there are no jury trials before then, but I need time to file motions before arraignment," she hissed.

"Fine, you can have more than thirty days, but I want to go to court before the end of July."

Chapter 11

Jaxson arched his eyebrows, watching the preliminary hearing. *That detective was lazy and didn't investigate anything. Jenna is rather good though. I know where I need to go from here.*

He drove to the scene of the crime—the Brown house. Jenna had Claire sign over her jail property which included the house keys. The house appeared mostly unchanged. The police released the crime scene, but the home couldn't enter probate until Claire's criminal case is closed. He first walked through the house to try to get a sense of what the family was like.

He took pictures of everything as always because you never knew what little thing might be significant. The wedding picture looked like it belonged in a bridal magazine. He noticed that many of the other photos seemed fake. Pictures of the little girl were everywhere. He found a room dedicated to sports memorabilia and Devon's awards. *Man, this guy was full of himself. How many newspaper articles and photos of yourself do you need?*

These people had way too much money. Ashley's room was every girl's dream. Stuffed animals, dolls, and doll houses lined the room. She had bookcases full of Laura Ingalls Wilder, Amelia Bedelia, Junie B. Jones, Beverly Cleary, Nancy Drew, and other book series. She had a pale pink carriage bed. Framed movie posters from Frozen, Tangled, and An American Girl hung on the walls.

In the master suite, he saw a king-sized bed, a four-piece bathroom, and multiple pictures of the family in different poses, including a large portrait of the couple on their wedding day. The hair on the back of his neck stood up as he looked around that bedroom and envisioned the violence that took place in there. Everything in the bathroom was in its place and the mother-in-law had the place cleaned, but it looked as if it always stayed that way. Things became neurotic when he entered the closet: each hanger was exactly an inch apart; every shoe precisely on the shelves without any dirt; purses, ties, and any of accessories were perfectly arranged as if for a catalogue. "These people took anal retentive to a whole other level," he said aloud.

He opened the drawers in the bedroom, and every one of them was full of heated, folded clothes. He found a journal of sorts in Claire's nightstand with writings. He read the first page and realized that it was an apology letter to Devon. He flipped through the pages and saw several more. He also found lists of things she was supposed to do. *Wow, this guy really was a piece of work.* He found a few other notepads and calendars and grabbed them all up. He found Claire's iPad and Devon's laptop and took both for forensic analysis.

Next, he walked around the whole house looking for any signs of violence. In the living room was a spot that had been repaired because the paint color was not exactly right and was not smooth and level with the rest of the wall. He found several nicks in the walls around the house—more than one would expect in this immaculate home. He found a crater in the wall of the master bedroom closet. The office door did not quite fit properly and did not match any other doors in the house. *It probably was destroyed and replaced.*

He looked around the place one more time and started to leave when he saw a box knocked over that had been behind an end table. He opened the box and found several broken pieces of jewelry, pictures ripped in half, and other little knickknacks. He had a gut feeling that these meant something, so he photographed them too.

He looked at the list of Claire's neighbors' names and knocked on all the neighbors' doors, but only one answered. A man in his seventies opened the door. "I already know Jesus, and I don't need to buy anything, son."

"That's good because I'm not selling anything and am not qualified to talk about Jesus. I'm an investigator for your neighbor Claire Brown. I was hoping to chat with you for a few minutes."

"The Browns. Tragedy."

"Yes, sir, did you know them well?"

"They kept to themselves. Would see them at the occasional neighborhood block party."

"What did you think of them?"

"The little girl was precious. I thought Devon was full of himself and didn't treat that pretty wife of his very well."

"In what way?"

"Nothing I can put my finger on exactly, but it was just the way he interacted with her. She seemed scared of him. He would make fun of her in front of people.

He always bragged about all of his accomplishments playing football and money his family had and that job."

"Did you ever hear or see any arguments?"

"No, but unless they were arguing outside, I probably wouldn't."

"What about injuries on Mrs. Brown?"

"She stayed inside most of the time, but one time I surprised her by bringing Ashley's ball back and she had a black eye."

"Here's my card. If you think of anything else or know anyone that has information, please give me a call."

"Thanks. I hope she's ok."

Chapter 12

Jenna walked into the local coffee shop and saw Jaxson sitting in the corner booth. "What have you got for me?"

"Hello to you too. Please sit down. I've got a laptop full of pictures of the house. I think there are a few things that could help prove an abusive relationship. We need to go through this stuff with the client. I also want to talk to this child. How do you want me to play that?"

She slid in the opposite side of the booth, dropping her bag down on the table. "What? Let's back up and go through one thing at a time, but no way Lara is going to allow that without a court order. The school won't let you either. I can subpoena the child to the trial or move for a deposition, but Claire insisted we leave her out of it. See if you can find a casual way to meet the grandmother and the child. Look into Devon's past. Let's see if he had any previous girlfriends."

"Why? Doesn't that concern you that she doesn't want you talking to the only other witness? I'm going to look for past girlfriends, but I'd also like to hear more from Claire about what happened and what we need to corroborate her story."

"You can go with me to see her tomorrow. In the meantime, I need to know more about the finances and if she had any motive to kill him other than the life insurance they brought up at prelim. Let me get some coffee and see what you've got."

She walked up to the counter and ordered a white chocolate mocha. When she returned, he had all his pictures on his laptop, and they went through each one.

When she seemed to have finished looking through everything, he asked, "So, what else do you do besides practice law?"

"Not much. Read, watch movies, play with my cat."

"Come on, you have to have a hobby or something you did before you became a defense lawyer."

"I used to sing and play the piano, but I don't really do that anymore."

"Why did you stop?"

"I don't normally talk about that."

"Relax, it's not like I'm going to blab it around town. You look like you could use a friend, and I admit, so could I."

She started cleaning the table up as she started talking. "While I was working on my music degree, I met Erik, and we hit it off right away. We performed duets at weddings. I played the piano for his solos. We starred in several theater productions. We did everything together. He proposed at a show we were in during the spring of our senior year. We had our wedding planned for that fall, but things changed." She paused for a minute, having nothing left to clean, rubbed sanitizer all over her hands, hoping he would leave it at that.

"Changed how?"

"You're not going to let this go, are you?" He shook his head. "Erik started having these extreme mood swings and became increasingly paranoid and depressed. When I'd ask him about it, he just kept saying that he was stressed."

"What happened?"

She twisted the ring on her finger, not looking at him. "Somehow, he got a gun and shot his neighbor across the street. He believed the guy was obsessed with me and was going to kill me. I found the gun and told the police. We found out he was schizoaffective—a type of schizophrenia—and eventually the Court found him not guilty by reason of mental illness and committed him to Oklahoma Forensic Center. While all of that was going on, I enrolled in law school. His public defender did such an excellent job, I wanted to be one. Erik blamed me and blocked me from his visitor list or being able to communicate. It broke my heart, and music just wasn't the same after that."

"Wow, sorry I didn't know it was going to be all of that. Have you dated since?"

"No, I thought he was the love of my life and clearly my judgment was off. I mean how do you not catch that your boyfriend of four years had schizophrenia? It's just safer to work."

"Ok, get up. It's time to go."

"Go where?"

"Enough real talk. Let's work the case."

"What do you mean?"

"I'm going to OU to interview people in the athletic department to find out about Devon. Come with me."

"I can't go. I've got things to do."

"What and why? Answer quickly before you make it up."

"I've got reports to read and motions to write."

"You can do both of those later, now come on." He pulled her up by the hand that was putting her legal pad notes back up in her bag.

"You're not giving me a choice, are you?" she asked.

"Nope, so let's go." He stood and started toward the door.

He stopped at a black BMW. "This is your car?"

"Yeah, you have something against BMWs?"

"No, I just thought you were a motorcycle guy."

"I have both."

Chapter 13

Jaxson and Jenna walked into the OU athletics building. Jaxson moseyed up to the front desk secretary. "Hi, I'm Jaxson Stone, and this is Jenna Miller. We need to find out background information about one of your former players, Devon Brown."

"How long ago?" The secretary barely looked up.

"About ten years ago."

"What sport?"

"Football."

"Most of the coaching staff has changed in that time, and we can't tell you much anyway. What is this about?"

"Mr. Brown was killed, and we are investigating everything."

"I'm not sure what we would know that would help you. You might start with the football communications people. They've been around for years. Third floor to the right."

"We will. Thanks."

As they entered the elevator, Jenna asked, "Do you really think anyone will tell us anything negative about him?"

"Depends. People love to gossip."

They exited the elevator and found one woman in her office with Air Pods in her ears and working steadily on a laptop. Jaxson slightly knocked on her door. "Miss, can we have a few minutes of your time?"

"What about? I'm on a deadline with this story," she stated, barely glancing in their direction.

"I'm Jenna Miller and I'm an attorney; this is my investigator Jaxson Stone. We are looking into the death of Devon Brown; did you know him?"

She sighed. "I'm A.J. I knew him. We were both 2010 graduates. Football isn't really my sport, but on the paper, I certainly covered football. I saw the latest news about what happened. What does his college life have to do with his death? I assume you represent his wife, am I right?"

"Maybe nothing, but we have to check out all angles."

"Anything specific you're looking for?"

"Actually yes, my client maintains that she acted in self-defense and that he was abusive and controlling throughout their relationship. I'd like to know if he had other girlfriends or if he ever got in trouble on campus for anything like that."

"I don't remember any official trouble, but you could check with campus security, but likely if there had been a real investigation, I would have heard about it. I recognized his wife from the pictures on the news because they were virtually inseparable his senior year, but I don't remember ever talking to her. She was just a freshman and shy and smitten if I remember right."

"Do you remember anyone before her?"

A.J. seemed to be thinking back. "I remember him with lots of dates, but I think there was one cheerleader he was with for quite a while...come to think about it, Darcie was her name, but she didn't graduate with us. We weren't close, so I don't know what happened."

"Did you ever hear any rumors about Devon? Trouble with girls or drinking or anything like that?"

"Nothing specific or any different than any of the other entitled players."

"Do you know anyone that we could talk to that might have known him or her personally?"

She thought for a moment. "We have a coach in special teams that I think was on the team with him, Derek Anderson; you might try him. Other than that, finding Darcie would be your best bet to know more about him."

"Thank you!" They both hollered and headed towards to the football offices looking for Derek.

"Derek?"

A hulk of a man stepped out. "Yeah, that's me. Who wants to know?"

"Jaxson Stone, and this is Jenna Miller. We are investigating the death of Devon Brown and wondering what you could tell us about him." He gave him a firm handshake.

"I haven't talked to him in ten years, how could I help?"

"Actually, we were wondering if you remember any Devon's girlfriends in college?"

"Devon was a player like many of the players, but I only remember two actual girlfriends: Claire and Darcie."

"Yes, do you remember Darcie's last name?"

He stopped sorting through the mail and looked at them. "Who do you work for?"

"I'm a public defender for Claire, his wife."

"I saw she was arrested for his murder, so why should I help a murderer?"

"I don't believe it was murder. I believe he was abusive, and she finally stood up for herself."

"Wish I could say I was shocked."

"Do you know about his abusing anyone else?"

"I work for the university, and they don't like bad press for the football program even for old players, so I don't want to be in the middle of anything and called to testify. So, can I talk to you off the record?"

"Yes, of course, I'm just trying to get information that might help my client."

"He had a quick temper and super controlling, so I could see him being that way, but I never knew of anything officially, but Darcie didn't come back for spring of sophomore year. That happens, but she also deleted her Facebook and stopped talking to any of her friends over that Christmas break. I was dating a cheerleader at that time too, and the whole squad was really upset."

"Do you remember her last name?"

"Uh, Johnson, I think."

"Derek, you've been a huge help. I promise we will leave you out of it. Did Devon ever say anything about why she didn't come back?"

"Only thing I ever heard him say was something like, 'She's crazy.' "

"Any idea where we might find her?" He asked.

"No, I haven't thought about her in years."

"Ok, thank you for your time." She shook his hand.

"Let's go to talk to the cheerleading department." He led the way and teased, "See, aren't you glad you came with me? We already have a lead.

"Ok, I'll give you that. How do you know where the cheerleading department is?"

"I have my ways: I can search for her in my databases. I think we can find her. Whether Darcie will talk to us is another story."

Jaxson approached the secretary. "Is Coach K in?"

"I'm not sure if she's available. Who should I say is asking?"

"Her nephew."

While the receptionist dialed a number, Jenna mouthed to him, "Nephew?"

He just smirked. "I have connections."

The receptionist announced, "Go on back."

They walked down a short hallway and turned into a large corner office when a petite, energetic female lunged toward him, "Jaxson! It's been too long. How are you?"

"I'm doing great KK." He picked the tiny woman up in a hug. "This is Jenna Miller, an attorney I'm working with. We're actually here on a case."

"Hi, just call me Coach K, everyone else does. Come on in and make yourself comfortable. Though I'm not sure how I could help." She indicated the chairs, smiled and shook Jenna's hand before sitting back at her desk.

"So, KK, Jenna is a public defender representing Claire Brown who is accused of murdering her husband Devon Brown, former football player here."

"I saw his murder on the news."

Jenna jumped in, "My client says Devon was abusive and that is what led to his death. We just talked to a football coach who graduated with him and said that he dated a cheerleader named Darcie Johnson prior to Claire and that she suddenly left school. Did you know her?"

"Yes, Darcie. Darcie and Devon were hot and heavy there for a while. She didn't come back spring of her sophomore year. We had our first practice after Christmas break, and she didn't show, which was not like her. The other girls said they hadn't seen her, and when we called her number, the phone went straight to voicemail. I looked her up on the computer and saw she had withdrawn, but she hadn't said a word to anyone. She was a talented cheerleader and a real sweetheart, and I hated to see her drop for no apparent reason, so I drove to her parents' house in Jenks.

"When she saw me, she broke into tears and couldn't talk. I asked her what happened, and she just kept saying, 'I can't go back there. I can't see him.' I asked her if she meant Devon, and she nodded. I tried to explain to her that first love hurts but that's no reason to transfer and that she would meet someone in no time.

"She shook her head and said, 'You don't understand, Coach K.' I asked her what she was going to do and told her she was too good to give up on cheerleading and anything else she wanted to do. She looked distraught but nodded and said she would figure something out, but not at OU. I tried to talk to her and her parents away from her, but her dad was adamant that she wasn't returning there. I suspected something traumatic happened, but never knew for sure."

"KK, do you have any idea where she may be now or ever hear what happened to her?" Jaxson asked.

"No, I sure don't. I hate to say it, but life moved on, and I don't know."

"Is there any way you could give us her parents' address? The one you visited?"

"I'm sorry, but I can't because it would violate

FERPA and could get me fired, but she went to Jenks High School if that helps you."

"I understand. Thank you so much for your help."

"Yes, KK, you've been a tremendous help." He hugged her goodbye.

"When are you going to come to a family dinner again? You can even bring her along if you like."

"We'll see, KK. Love you though."

"You too, Jaxson. Be good. Keep him in line, Jenna. It was nice to meet you."

"Same with you!" They left her office and started the walk back to his car in between all the college students hurrying to and from class.

"Slow down, Jaxson. I'm in heels," Jenna yelled.

"Aren't you always?"

"Not if I were planning to walk a couple miles."

He slowed his pace until she caught up with him. "Why don't you take your shoes off then?"

"And walk on this dirty pavement in bare feet? No, thank you!"

Chapter14

The next day, Jenna and Jaxson went to the jail to visit Claire. Jaxson arranged all the pictures on the table before the jailers brought her in.

Claire eyed the stranger, looking from the guard to Jaxson and to her lawyer. "Who's this?"

"This is my investigator Jaxson. He went inside your home and took pictures. We have several follow-up questions. We are trying to corroborate your story."

"You still don't believe me?"

"It's not about what I believe. It's what I can prove. The police didn't do a thorough investigation and, so far, we have nothing to present other than your word."

"I need a lawyer that believes me and is going to fight for me. This is about my daughter! Have you done anything about getting her away from Lara?"

"Claire, I do believe in you, but that is not the point. My job as a lawyer is to zealously defend you and represent you, and that is what I am doing. I am not your custody attorney, nor have I been appointed by the court to be your custody attorney, but if you are sentenced to life in prison your daughter is going to stay with Lara, so let's keep our eye on the ball."

She looked down at the pictures and picked one up. "Where did you find these?"

Jaxson answered, "I accidentally knocked over this

box; they were hidden in the living room. I just thought it was odd. What are these?"

"Things of mine that he broke or hid from me as punishment. The broken bracelet was a sixteenth birthday present from my mom and sister. The picture was of me and my best friend growing up and her brother."

"Look through the other pictures; tell us anything else that stands out?"

"This patch in the wall is from an argument. This was when Ashley was about one. She had been sick and up crying a lot. Devon and I had a nice dinner and were watching a movie and he was in a romantic mood. I fell asleep, and he just lost it. He grabbed me up by the arms and screamed in my face, 'I try to spend time with you and do something nice, and you don't even have the decency to stay awake.' I told him I was just tired from Ashley being sick. He threw me into the wall and said, 'You're just worthless. All you do is stay home and take care of Ashley; you shouldn't be that tired.' "

"Claire, can you give us any specific dates of any of the physical violence occurred? I want to try to find any independent witnesses that can testify for you?" He took notes.

"That's like asking someone for every date they ever had sex. I don't remember specific dates or times for most of them, but I do remember one time when we went on a trip with his mother for the 4th of July. He was mad because I wasn't getting food out quickly enough, and he punched me in the stomach. His mom walked in on at the tail end of it, and when Devon walked away, she looked at me and said, 'You should really work on not setting him off,' like it was my fault."

"And you never went to the hospital or doctor for any injuries?"

"Yes, a couple of times, but never told the truth. Has anyone talked to my daughter?"

"No, we can subpoena her, but without knowing what she is going to say, I'm concerned."

"What about the letter Ash wrote me that talked about Devon being mean to me?"

"It's hearsay. We can call her as a witness and introduce it, but on its own, it doesn't help me."

"Describe the way the stabbing went down again. Honestly, the fact that you stabbed him in the back will be the hardest for a jury to believe."

Claire demonstrated as well as she could while having one wrist chained to the bench where she sat. "It all happened so fast. It's hard to describe. He had me pinned up against the counter with his hands around my throat and squeezing. I frantically looked around and tried to maneuver out of his grasp, but he was too strong. I was reaching for something to hit him with, and I felt the knife that I had been cutting vegetables with and grabbed the handle and just stabbed. It took what felt like forever for him to let go, and he had this shocked look on his face as he fumbled for a second and then fell. I was too shocked and scared to move for a minute, but then bent down and felt for a pulse and to see if he was breathing, but didn't find either, so I jumped up and ran across the kitchen to call 911."

"We should work on a demonstration or an expert that can recreate this and show the jury that your story is plausible."

"I agree, and the domestic violence expert is

coming on Friday to interview you. Tell her the whole truth. This is part of the work product of our defense, so she cannot speak unless we authorize her to do so. She is part of our team. We are working for you. Also, did you know about Devon's ex-girlfriend Darcie?"

"He mentioned that she had a breakdown and left school. Why?"

"Well, Jaxson and I went and dug around at OU and talked to a few people on staff who remembered that they were serious, and suddenly she cut off all contact with all of her friends at OU and didn't come back. We spoke with the cheerleading coach who went and met with her after she left, and she got the impression that something bad happened. If she would confirm that he was abusive to her as well, that would be huge for our case."

"I hadn't ever thought about her. He probably was." Claire sighed. "I can't believe I'm here. I had a bright future. He ruined my life, but I won't regret it because I had Ashley. I have to get her back. She's what I'm fighting for." Her voice rose in both pitch and volume toward the end of her monologue.

"I know, trust me, I'm working my best for you, but just remember I have about 300 other cases I'm also working on, which is why it's not possible for me to meet with you every week or update you all the time, but I am and will do my best. Stay strong!"

She hit the buzzer to let the guards know that they were finished with their meeting. As she and Jaxson packed up, Jaxson showed his pictures of the kitchen to Claire. "Can you just point out exactly where the altercation took place?"

"This is where he had me pinned to the counter.

Here is where the knife was, and here is where he fell."
Claire pointed to various spots in the pictures.

The guard arrived then. "I'll walk you out."

They exited and Jaxson said, "I believe her. Her story makes sense."

"I do too, but I worry about confirmation bias."

"What?"

"It's basically where you think one thing or want to think it and then you take everything else you learn and make it fit to your original thought, whether it does or not."

"Ah, I see, but we are getting information that backs up our belief that she was battered and killed in self-defense. I'm going to find Darcie. That's my focus now."

Chapter 15

On the ride back to the jail, Claire couldn't help but remember that day at the insurance agent's office. It was the week after Ashley was born.

Devon said, "Claire, you're a mother now. Think about her. What if something happens to me, you will need the money to take care of her or, heaven forbid we both die in a car accident, she needs to be able to live a comfortable life."

It was his ridiculous idea to get these policies, and now they were using it against her as if she murdered him for the money. Anyone who has watched television knows murderers can't collect life insurance. *Who am I kidding? I never planned on killing him. I always just kept hoping the good times would return.*

After the "baby moon" stage ended, Devon's moods returned. When she told Devon she was pregnant, he was ecstatic. He brought her breakfast in bed. He was kind and attentive. A bit controlling over what she could and couldn't do and eat, but he was so excited about the prospect of having a little girl that even when he was in a terrible mood, he looked at her with love for the child she was carrying. If reality had only been as good as his fantasy, but raising a child is work. She was up with Ashley every couple of hours either soothing her crying or breastfeeding. She was tired all the time and didn't keep herself up or pay attention to Devon as much as she did before.

She remembered the first day his attitude changed. He came home and sneered, "Another day in your sweats, no makeup, and no dinner. You used to take pride in your appearance. I wouldn't even touch you looking like that. No wonder men have mistresses. Get your act together!"

"I'm sorry, I'm just exhausted. Can we order something in for dinner or go out?"

"Go out? You must have lost your mind? I wouldn't be caught dead out in public with you the way you look now."

"I would get cleaned up. It would be nice to get out of the house."

"I'll take you out when you deserve it. Besides, the baby will cry anyway. Now get something easy prepared and on the table for dinner."

Once Ashley started talking, he gave all his love and affection to her more and more. He ignored Claire except when he wanted to have sex or when he had an audience, but he doted on Ashley. He made fun of her in front of their daughter but always claimed he was joking. He would blatantly say that she was lucky to have found him or she would be completely lost and stuck in that trailer park.

In private, he constantly told her how no one else would love her or put up with her craziness, but it was coolness and lack of affection that hurt the most. She planned romantic dinners and greeted him with a kiss, but he brushed her off. He refused to hold her hands or cuddle, unless it was part of a show, or he was in the mood. She begged him to love her, and he made her feel worthless.

Her marriage was dead, so she lived for Ashley. She stayed home with her and, once she started pre-K, she was the classroom mom, a PTA volunteer, chaperone for field trips—whatever she could to be with her. She would never leave Devon because of her. He would make her life hell. He always threatened, "You can leave, but if you walk out that door, I'll make sure you don't see Ashley again." He also loved to say, "The vow was 'until death do us part' and that's the only way you'll get out."

She prayed, "Dear God, I know I have my faults, but please help me out of this. Not for me, but for Ashley."

She was almost asleep when the guard threw her a letter. She nearly ripped the envelope apart to get to it. "It's from Ashley!" She couldn't help but shout to anyone who might be listening. *Aw, her handwriting has improved so much over the last few months. She's so smart; her test scores showed her years ahead.*

Momma, I miss you so much. I hate it here. I have to go to all these parties and stuff at the club, but I made a friend and she helped me with this. Her name is Lizzie. Nana got me a dog. His name is Zeus. He's so awesome.

You are the best mom in the world. I miss you sooo much! You shouldn't be in there. Daddy was mean to you, but I miss him. Are you ok? I don't know what jail is like. When will you get to come home? Nana took your pictures down. I snuck one in my room. You've got to come rescue me. I want to go back home. I love you! Ash.

The picture she drew of Zeus was just adorable. Claire couldn't stop the sobs that racked her. When she finally gained her composure, she called her mom and told her about the letter.

"That's great, honey! I have court on Monday to fight for visitation."

"Wonderful! Please let me know. When you get to see her, tell her how much I love her and miss her."

Chapter 16

Jaxson researched all his different databases: Truthfinder, LexisNexis, social media, and anything else he could think of relating to Darcie Johnson. He found that her parents moved the same year that Darcie quit OU. On Saturday morning, he made the turnpike trek to Tulsa and was surprised to learn as he got closer that they lived in a gated community. His research showed that while the parents had good jobs, they couldn't afford a half a million-dollar home. They either lived above their means or had money coming in other than from their jobs. He rang the doorbell, and a woman in her fifties answered the door. "Hi, can I help you?"

"Are you Mrs. Johnson?"

"Who's asking?"

"I'm Jaxson Stone and I'm a private investigator," showing her his badge and giving her a couple minutes to look at it, "May I have a few minutes of your time?"

"What is this about? What are you investigating?"

"I work for Claire Brown, who is charged with murdering her husband, Devon Brown. We understand that your daughter Darcie was a former girlfriend of his. I'm gathering background information on him. The news portrays him as the OU football hero, but that's not who he was."

The woman's eyes widened. "Look, I feel sorry for

that woman, and he certainly had another side, but we can't help you."

"Can't or won't?" The woman put her hands in her pocket and looked away.

Just then a man's voice boomed, "Both. Now you need to leave."

"Mr. Johnson, I presume, if I could just have five minutes of your time."

"No, sir. We can't help you," he barked and shut the door.

Jaxson left his card on the door hoping they would change their minds.

He called Jenna, and she answered on the second ring. "Hey, any luck?"

"No. Mrs. Johnson seemed like she maybe wanted to help but said she can't. Then, Mr. Johnson came to the door and told me to get off his property, but I was going to tell you one thing that was strange was that they have modest jobs, but they moved to this huge home in a gated community in the summer of 2008 right after Darcie left. I wonder if they got a payout or something. I'll keep digging and I will find her one way or another."

"I'll look for any court records. I just looked under Devon, but I'll search for her as well. Maybe she changed her name or got married."

"Ok, I'll holler at you later."

****

As he backed into his driveway, his phone rang with the screen showing "Unknown." He answered, "Hello?"

"Is this Jaxson Stone?"

"It is. Who is this?"

"This is Darcie. My parents told me you were at their house earlier today asking questions about me. I don't appreciate that. I have put him behind me and don't care to think about it again." Her voice had a tremulous tone.

"Ma'am, I don't know what you went through, but I do know what Claire Brown went through, and it ended with her having to kill him. She's in jail on murder charges, and Devon's mother has custody of her daughter. The prosecution and media acts as if Devon were a great guy and she killed him for his money. I bet you know who the real Devon was and that you can help us."

After an appreciable silence on the other end, he looked down at the phone to see if she had disconnected, but she was still there. "Darcie? I'm not trying to bring up painful memories, but you may be the only person other than Claire that knows the real him."

"She had a daughter with him?"

"Yes, she's six years old."

"And Lara is raising her?"

"As of right now because she has been charged with killing him. Lara has a lot more money than Claire's family."

"I would hate to have Lara raise someone else."

"Then, help us out here. I work for Claire's attorney. She's a public defender named Jenna Miller. Can we come meet with you in person?"

"I live in Dallas. I would like to help you, but my parents and I signed a non-disclosure agreement."

"Do you have a copy of it?"

"My parents do."

"Can you email it to me? I'll text you my e-mail

address. Wait! I don't have your number. Jenna would be better able to talk to you about that. So, can we come meet with you?"

"I don't know. I'm concerned that I broke the agreement just by telling you about it."

"Why don't I have Jenna call you? She's the attorney and can talk to you about that."

"Ok, I'm texting you my number. I'll try to get the agreement to send to you."

He heard the text tone. "Sounds good. Thanks."

"Bye."

He immediately dialed Jenna. "I'm beginning to think you have no other friends."

"Guess who just called me?"

"Who?"

"Darcie."

"What did she say?"

"At first she yelled at me for bothering her parents and that she had put that chapter behind her. Then, after a little bit she seemed sympathetic, particularly to the fact that Lara is raising Claire's daughter. She said that she and her parents signed a non-disclosure agreement, and she was afraid she broke it just by telling me that much. She is supposed to send me a copy of it for you to look at and for you to call her."

"That's great news. I would imagine the non-disclosure agreement would end with his death. Where is she?"

"She said that she lives in Dallas. I've sent her my e-mail for her to forward that contract. I'll shoot it to you as soon as I get it."

"Good work!"

"So, you know this may require us to take a little

trip down to Dallas?"

"What? I don't have time to go to Dallas."

"This could be a huge witness for you. She will need your reassurance. We can leave on a Friday afternoon. You can't work every weekend anyway and take a little break from work while down in Dallas. It wouldn't kill you."

"We'll see."

"Later."

Chapter 17

Jenna had one of those all-day felony dockets where she was completely drained at the end. When she walked into Rose's house with dinner, she kicked her wedges off and set the table.

"Jenna, thanks for bringing dinner over. I can taste today and want to eat. How was your day?"

"Long. I lost count of how many plea forms I did in a row. I also had several revocations and sentencing hearings too. I didn't think it was ever going to end. The clients today were infuriating."

"Ah, but you love it. You would be bored without them!"

"True. A guy today told me that the meth in his car wasn't his even though he was a drug dealer, but when he carries stuff with him, he keeps it in a sock attached to himself, so you can't tell anything extra is there."

"Creative. What did you say to that?"

"I told him that in no way was I arguing that to a jury."

"How's your murder case going?"

"Jaxson may have gotten a real lead for us. So, I'm feeling hopeful."

"Who is Jaxson?"

"I thought I told you. He's my investigator on this case. I didn't care for him at first, but he's good at his job." She couldn't help the grin that came over her face.

"So, tell me more about this guy?"

"Not much to tell. We're just working together."

"Right."

"We may have to go to Dallas together to interview a crucial witness though."

"Overnight trip I assume?"

"Probably would be a long day, but it's not like that. We would definitely have two rooms."

"You need to live a little, Jenna. Life can't be all about work."

"Funny, that's what he said too."

****

She was almost asleep when her phone dinged with a text from Jaxson. "Check your e-mail. She sent the NDA."

"Thanks." She grabbed her iPad and opened the NDA. She read through all the language and while most of it is the typical boilerplate language, if breached, the damages requiring paying the entire settlement back or $750,000. *No wonder they are worried about breaching. Most contracts are voided with the death of one of the parties. I mean you can't defame a dead person.*

She texted Jaxson again. "Send me her number. I'm going to call her tomorrow. Are you busy this weekend?"

"Not for you. Are we making a trip to Dallas?"

"Maybe."

"I knew you'd come around."

****

The phone rang two, three times. Finally, on the fourth ring a disembodied voice answered, "Hello."

"Hi Darcie, this is Jenna, Claire Brown's attorney.

I believe you talked to my investigator the other day."

"Yes, did you get the non-disclosure agreement?"

"I reviewed it last night and, while it is pretty standard, Devon is dead. It would be difficult for them to enforce that contract against you."

"You don't know these people. They are brutal. Lara would sue just for spite."

"Right, and it is that woman who is raising Claire's daughter right now. Don't do it for me or Claire, but for Ashley, an innocent six-year-old girl."

"What if she sues me? My parents spent that money on a house and paying for my college and graduate school."

"I promise that I or a friend of mine will represent you pro bono. There's more than money at stake here. So can Jaxson and I come and meet with you this weekend?"

"I guess so. I'm just scared. I've done my best to move past these people."

"Devon is dead, Darcie. He can't hurt you anymore. I promise that we will protect you."

"You just don't know how evil that woman is. She appears sweet, but if you don't do what she wants, she will make you pay."

"I understand. Let's talk about everything this weekend!"

After her phone call, she retrieved her papers from her box and found her fax from the domestic violence expert. The summary of the report read: "While Ms. Brown has definitely experienced trauma and while she acknowledges some of her victimization at the hands of her husband, she still is in denial about the state and level of dysfunction in her life. Her goal still seems to be protecting her daughter rather than caring about herself. She almost seems disconnected from herself and in conversations normalizes the abuse. She suffers from severe anxiety and heightened sensitivity as is common with survivors of intimate partner violence. She is a prime candidate for the battered woman's defense." The rest of it breaks down the interview and test scores.

She texted Jaxson. "Darcie is on board. I'm about to book a couple rooms. Do you need a smoking room or anything special?"

"No, I don't smoke, and I'm not a control freak."

"I'll leave work by noon on Friday, and we can leave any time after that."

"I'll drive, but you owe me dinner, and I'm not a cheap date just so you know."

"Yeah, we'll see. In other good news, the report from the expert supports our case strategy."

Chapter 18

Jenna's largest rollaway luggage was on the front porch when Jaxson pulled up. As he loaded the bag in the truck he said, "You do realize this is just an overnight trip, right?"

"Look, I just don't like to be without anything I might need."

"Right, control freak." She started to say something, but he interrupted, "Don't even try to say you're not."

She adjusted the seat until she was comfortable and pulled out the latest Phillip Margolin novel and started reading. "You don't get enough of the legal world at work?"

"Leave me alone. I love my legal thrillers."

"You couldn't just talk to me on the drive?"

"Sorry, I figured you would want to listen to music and focus on driving. It's nothing personal. I always read on trips if I don't have to drive. If I am driving, I listen to an audiobook."

"Suit yourself then."

Great. I've offended him. This is why I don't have friends. I wasn't meaning to. I just like to read. Why does he have to give me such a hard time about everything?

When they were almost to Turner Falls, he asked, "Want to stop for something to drink?"

She jumped and squealed, "What?"

He laughed at her. "Geez. Jumpy much? Just asked if you wanted to stop for a drink."

"I was just absorbed in the book. Sorry, but yes a drink sounds great."

****

Around 4:00, they pulled into the Crowne Plaza where she had made reservations. He let her off at the door to check them in, and he parked and brought their luggage in. She handed him his key. "You're in 608. I'm in 603. WIFI password is written inside."

"Thanks. So, I drove, where are you taking me to dinner later?"

"You're being paid for this little trip, are you looking for double compensation?" she asked with a laugh.

"I'm not going to bill you for drive time and per diem. Just buy my dinner. What do you like to eat? I can look up the best places to go."

"I hadn't even thought about dinner yet, but something we don't have in OKC. Something with a variety on the menu. I'm going to go relax for a while."

"Ok, I'll come by at 7."

She went into her hotel room that had the typical king size bed, compact fridge, desk, but overlooking the Dallas skyline. She changed into her swimsuit and went down to the pool area. As she settled into the jacuzzi with her next book she saw Jaxson swimming laps. *Dang, he's better looking without a shirt.*

He caught her staring and smirked, "Like what you see?" Then he joined her.

She knew she was blushing bright red. "I was just surprised to see you. It seemed like you were doing a routine."

"I swam in high school and college. So, you really are a bookworm, you brought a book to the hot tub."

"Why do you insist on picking on me? I'm usually by myself so I keep myself occupied in my books."

"Lighten up, killer. Wait, is that a different one that what you were reading in the car?"

"Yeah, I finished that one. I'm just starting this one. It's the latest Mary Higgins Clark one. She is writing this series with a co-author about a TV producer investigating unsolved cases."

"I see, well I'll let you get back to it."

"It's ok. It may get wet anyway. So, I've noticed you sure ask me a lot of questions, but you avoid talking about yourself. So, no wife or kids at home missing you this weekend?"

"I'm divorced."

"That's all you're going to tell me? What happened? Who wanted the divorce?"

"No one goes into marriage wanting or expecting a divorce, but she had a problem with the 'forsaking all others' vow."

"I'm sorry. That's hurtful."

"I let her get away with murder before I finally threw up my hands. I caught her in bed with her last affair in our bed. She had the most extreme mood swings. One psychiatrist diagnosed her as having both bipolar disorder and borderline personality disorder after one of her suicide attempts."

"One of her suicide attempts?"

"Yes, when she didn't get her way, she would cut herself or take a bottle of pills to manipulate me or her parents. After I caught her cheating that last time and told her I was done, she started the car in the garage. She was unconscious, but alive, when I got there. She hedged her bets and sent a suicide video over text to me, her mother, and her latest boy toy. She thought for sure I wouldn't divorce her in that condition."

"Sorry. I guess we both picked people with problems. How long were you with her?"

"High school sweethearts. I didn't know any different back then. We started dating at sixteen, married at nineteen. Finally divorced at twenty-seven. I've stayed single since."

Jenna's phone rang then, and she grabbed the towel she purposefully put nearby wiped her hands off and answered, "Hi, this is Jenna."

"Jenna, it's Darcie."

"Hey, we are here in Dallas. Are we still on for nine in the morning?"

"Yes, but I decided that I would rather you all come to my house. This is very personal, and I would rather not talk about it in a public place, or at least not now."

"Of course, wherever you feel comfortable."

"I'll text the address."

"See you in the morning!" Jenna pulled herself up out of the jacuzzi and wrapped a towel around her. "Well, if you're still wanting to do dinner, I need to head back to my room and get ready. You better find a good place."

Chapter 19

A couple hours later they were sitting at Papa Bros. Steakhouse and eating salads. "This is a pretty nice place you picked Jaxson."

"The hotel guide highly recommended it, and it's been too long since I had a good steak."

"You were teasing me about working all the time. What about you? What do you do when not investigating?"

"I do triathlons."

"Really? I like to run but haven't done any races."

"Yeah. I've done three so far and do most local runs and bike races. I've done the last three OKC Memorial Marathons."

"How did you do?"

"Last one I finished in three hours."

"That's impressive!"

"Thanks. How much do you run?"

"I try to run four to six miles a day." They continued to talk about random subjects. *I could talk to him all night. So odd, I don't normally like people.*

The waitress came back. "Here's your check when you're ready." Jaxson grabbed the ticket, pulled out a credit card, and placed it in the fold.

"You don't need to do that. This is work, you know."

"Work. Right. Just work. An expense then."

She sensed that she had wounded him again. *What is your problem? You couldn't just leave it at you don't have to do that.* "I just meant…"

"I know what you meant," he snapped. "I'll get the car. Grab my card when she brings it back."

Am I always this catty? I used to be a nice person. What happened? She saw the dinner cost him $100 with the twenty percent tip. Should I apologize or what?

She got in the passenger side wondering what to say. Thankfully, he broke the silence. "You ready to go back to the hotel or want check out the local scene?"

"It's only 8:30. We can go somewhere else if you want. What did you have in mind?"

"You'll have to wait and see."

He drove them around for a while, hearing "In a half mile, turn left." Then, "Continue for three miles." Eventually, they arrived at One Nostalgia Tavern. It was typical western bar with wooden tables, bar tops, and casual atmosphere. The sound of live off-key karaoke greeted them as they walked in. She followed him toward a table in the back.

"You brought me to a karaoke bar?"

"Thought you might want to get back into singing."

"Here?"

"Why not? Do you want a beer?"

"Nah. Just a water, thanks!"

He left the bar. She played her Best Fiends game while he did that. She began to wonder if he had ditched her at this point because he'd been gone awhile.

"Is that one of those story and puzzle games?"

"Yeah, it's good for preventing Alzheimer's."

"Exactly how old are you?"

"Thirty-one. You?"

"Thirty-three. Aren't you a little young to worry about that?"

Before she could answer, she heard the DJ say, "Up next singing 'Tennessee Whiskey' is Jaxson."

He bolted up on stage, and her mouth dropped to the floor when she heard his smooth baritone voice. Her heart stirred in a way it hadn't in a decade. He shot her a sly smile. Watching and listening to him, she was practically drooling. She strained to hear over the noisy drunks. When the second chorus came around, she could swear he was singing it to her, but why would he?

He came back to the table with smirk on his face. "I forgot to tell you that my other hobby is playing guitar and singing in a cover band."

"You are talented. I was not expecting that."

"I'm looking forward to hearing you soon."

"I don't know what I would sing."

"Don't worry, I signed you up, and you're on after this girl."

"What song? What if I don't know it?"

"Trust me, you'll know it. You'd have to have been on another planet. It was a huge hit in the 90s."

"I haven't sung in public in a long time."

"I know; you told me. Don't you think it's time to move on?"

The DJ came back on and said, "Coming up next is Jenna with 'How Do I Live?' "

Her heartbeat raced through her whole body. She bent over and grabbed the table with one hand to steady herself. Then she ambled toward the front. *What if I make a fool of myself after he did so well? At least I know the song.* The music started and she sang softly at first, but her tone and volume took on a new energy.

88

Adrenaline was pumping so she focused on a clock in the back and over the heads of the people in the crowded bar. The crowd erupted in applause.

She darted back to the table, her head down.

"Killer has a set of pipes," he said when she slid in the chair across from him.

"I'll take that as a compliment, I guess." She shrugged her shoulders.

"And you had fun, I could tell."

With a slight grin on her face, she said, "Little bit."

"Ok, you up for a duet or a dance before we head back?"

"I can't remember the last time I danced."

"Dancing it is." He grabbed her hand and pulled her along behind him to the dance floor. Luke Bryan's "Play It Again" came on the radio, which was perfect because it was fun one. Then they lined danced to a Garth Brooks song. Then, Dan & Shay's "Speechless" came on, and they slow danced to that.

What is going on with me? My heart is beating like crazy. Admit it to yourself. You like this guy. He's not looking to be in a relationship, or certainly not with me. I've got to stop this. Not sure I would survive another heartbreak. As the song ended, she abruptly pulled back and said, "We probably better get back."

"Yeah, sure."

They drove back to the hotel in companionable silence. When they were about to get off on the elevator he said, "Tonight was fun."

"It was, and thank you, I needed that." The elevator dinged then, and he signaled for her to walk ahead. As they walked to her door, she asked, "Why don't we have breakfast in the hotel restaurant around eight before we meet Darcie?"

"All right. See you in the morning." He lingered for a second, and their eyes locked. The silence was too awkward for her, and she fidgeted, grabbing the key card and putting it in the door. As she pushed the door open, she glanced back at him. "Well, good night."

He tilted his head but reached up and stroked her cheek. "Sweet Dreams."

Way to screw that up, girl. He might have been interested, but when you shut him down multiple times in one night, he's not going to keep trying. Particularly not a guy that looks like that, and despite first impressions, seems to be a good man. But then maybe I'm imagining it. He could get any girl he wanted. Why would he want me?

Chapter 20

The hotel wake-up call jerked Jaxson awake. He rubbed his eyes. *Ugh. I need more sleep. Couldn't sleep for trying to figure out this dang woman. She's the queen of mixed signals, but then again why do I care so much? This is why I'm done with the whole relationship thing. This chick is complicated and certainly not a friend with benefits type. I don't need this.*

****

After hitting the snooze button about three times, Jenna finally rolled out of bed. She was exhausted because she tossed and turned all night before thinking about Jaxson. *Focus. This is work. This interview with Darcie may be the key for saving Claire.* She took a long, hot shower, and dressed in a business casual outfit, packed her things, and went down to breakfast with Jaxson; however, neither one of them had much to say to each other.

****

They pulled into a gated community, lined with shrubs on the outside with about thirty condos each complete with landscaping, a garage, and a sidewalk. They drove around and found Darcie's. "This is a pretty ritzy area. I wonder how she affords it," Jaxson said as they pulled in the drive.

"It really is. This should be an interesting interview."

They walked up to the red door and rang the doorbell. Almost immediately, a tall and thin woman with long caramel color hair coming down to her shoulders answered the door. "Hi. You must be Jenna and Jaxson."

"Yes. Thanks for seeing us."

"Sure. Come on in."

Darcie was skinny with curves in the right places, a perky smile with perfect teeth, and long wavy hair cascading down. Jenna's eyes moved to the brightly colored abstract paintings on the walls and the bookcases full of books and the modern club couches. Darcie motioned for them to sit.

"Darcie, do you mind if we record this conversation?" Jaxson asked as he pulled his phone out.

She shook her head.

"Darcie, I know this must be difficult, but can you tell us about your relationship with Devon?" Jenna asked.

"First, I want to say that meeting Devon changed my life. We were freshmen. We saw each other that fall but didn't really talk other than in passing. In the spring though, we were in the same English class, and he immediately started flirting with me. We went out on our first date that first weekend of spring semester. He took me to a fancy restaurant in downtown OKC. He impressed me with roses, candy, balloons. I was obsessed. I couldn't stop daydreaming about him, stalking his Facebook profile, imagining our life together. I rarely had a chance to miss him because he was always around. Looking back on it, it was obsession and possession."

"What exactly do you mean?"

"He always wanted me with him. It was a heady feeling: being wanted and needed like that. He showered me with attention: calls, texts, and e-mails throughout the day if we were apart. He took me home to see his parents regularly and made it clear that we had a future together. He wanted to impress me. They had money—lots of it. I grew up in a middle-class family and lived a comfortable life, but they were not millionaires by a long shot. They even took me on vacation with them that summer. His mother made it clear that I would be a perfect trophy wife and that was what she required."

Jaxson asked, "When did things go wrong?"

"Looking back, little alarms sounded. He always had to do the talking and ordered me around and was condescending to me in a way that he played off as funny. My parents thought we were too serious. He would show up if I went home or went out with my friends without him, but I was so in love with him that I didn't care. I thought I was the luckiest person in the world. He always had to get his way and was very demanding but had a way of manipulating me into thinking it was my idea. Sometimes it got on my nerves, and we had little arguments, but I always gave in to him, and usually he would reward me with jewelry or a special date."

"Darcie, I get the sense that there's more to it than this," she prodded.

Her face turned red, and her smile turned downward. "Yes, but even after all these years, it is still hard to talk about. It was the last day of the fall semester of our sophomore year. We went to a party at his fraternity house. It was a typical party: cram packed with drinking and dancing. I thought we were just having fun like every other party, but Devon drank more than usual that night. A bunch of us were talking dancing, and joking. I didn't think anything about it, but Devon got this look on his face like I'd never seen before. He grabbed me around the arm and dragged me up the stairs to his room. I asked, 'Devon, what's wrong?' His only answer was to squeeze my arm tighter. When we got to his room, he locked the door and slapped me so fast and hard that I fell.

"I was so stunned I couldn't move. Then, he thrust me backward until my back hit the back wall. He hovered in my face screaming, 'How dare you embarrass me like that? Just who do you think you are?' I said, 'Dev, what are you talking about?' He yelled again, 'You're supposed to by my girl, and you were all over Josh. Flirting and carrying on like a slut.' He put one hand around my throat and started squeezing. I started losing my breath, but then he let me go and asked, 'Are you sorry?' I told him that I didn't mean to hurt him and that it wouldn't happen again or something like that. He let go of me for a minute and took another long drink of beer."

Tears dripped out of Darcie's eyes, her lip quivered, and she covered her face with her hands. Jaxson and she looked at each other sensing that she wasn't finished. You could hear a pin drop in her living room.

"Then, he said, 'Well you better make it up to me. You know what I want.' He sat down on the bed and signaled for me to get on my knees. I couldn't imagine what more he would do to me if I didn't, so I got down, but I was too scared to focus, and he kept gagging me.

In an instant, I was on my stomach on the bed, and he yanked my dress up. I pleaded, 'No. Not like this. You're hurting me.' He entered me from behind and when I started to cry out in pain, he pushed my head down in the pillow and whispered, 'Don't make a sound.' It seemed like time slowed down and it took forever." She exhaled.

She reached for Darcie's hand and whispered, "I'm so sorry. We brought this all back up."

"You didn't. It's not something you get over. It changed my life, but I don't tell the whole story very often. I am a licensed practical counselor now. I specialize in working with women and children who have been abused or sexually assaulted."

"What a fantastic way to turn a traumatic event into something good."

"What happened afterward?"

"He made me shower with him and kept me there in his room until the morning."

Jaxson interrupted then. "I hate to pepper you with questions, but did you file a report?"

"I guess I should finish the story. The next morning when we woke up, I put my clothes on and acted like everything was fine and told him I had to finish getting my things and get home because my parents were expecting me. He was hungover and let me go and said he would call me later. I went back to my dorm and called Campus Police. They didn't take me seriously and just said this was just a typical morning after regrets. The truth was they knew he was a football player and that his parents were big donors to the University. I raced home and, as soon as I saw my mom, I just broke down in tears. She took me to the hospital for a rape kit and they documented my injuries. I knew he had ripped me because I bled forever, but they didn't find his DNA because he made me shower. My father was livid and called our local police, but they said they couldn't do anything because it happened in Norman.

"After I left the hospital, I went into my room, closed all the blinds, and kept a sleep mask to avoid the light. I just slept. I didn't eat. If I went into the bathroom, I looked for pills to swallow. Meanwhile, Devon called my phone back-to-back and then would fire off ten or twenty texts and start calling again. I blocked his number, and then, he started calling my parents' home.

"I heard my father answer, 'Don't call here again. If I have anything to do with it, you will rot in jail.'

"The next day Devon pounded and yelled through my window, 'Darcie, get your ass out here and talk to me. You're seriously pissing me off.' Officers came and told him to leave. A nice female officer helped me fill out an emergency protective order and called the judge on a weekend to get an emergency order. When the officer left and my parents finally left my room, I swallowed a bottle of my mom's Ativan." Darcie finally looked back up at them.

"That's awful. I'm so glad you are okay. So, he was never arrested for rape or domestic violence?"

She rubbed the back of her neck and blew out a breath. "No, Devon's father came to see my parents after that and brought a non-disclosure agreement and a cashier's check for $750,000. His dad guaranteed Devon would never come near me again if I dismissed the emergency protective order and signed off on having it sealed. I was in the hospital and didn't care about anything else, so my parents told me to sign and take the money. My counselor recommended that I delete all my social media accounts, change my number, delete my email address; anything that he knew, I changed. I even moved down to Dallas with my aunt because I was afraid that he would never leave me alone. The next fall, I enrolled at SMU with their money and even was able to get a master's with the money and scholarships."

No one spoke for a moment, and an awkward silence followed. Darcie, unable to sit still, walked into the kitchen. They heard ice dropping into glasses. Darcie brought in a tray and announced, "I needed tea. I hope you all like sweet tea."

"Never say no to that," Jaxson answered and grabbed a glass.

She took a drink and asked, "Darcie, are you willing to come up and testify about these things?"

Her head dropped into her hands, and she shook. "I was afraid of that. I really don't want to, but I understand another woman's life is at stake, as well as her daughter's. I wouldn't want Lara Brown to raise another child. She made it clear that I wasn't in the same league as her son, but if I was going to be with him, I needed to make him happy. She was all about appearances and their reputation, a narcissist in the truest sense of the word. The world revolved around her, and she had to have her way. Devon learned it firsthand."

"Claire is terrified of that and is all she talks about. Even more than her trial or concern about going to prison, so can we count on you?"

"If you need me, I will do my best to come through."

Jaxson asked, "I have a few specific questions so I can follow up. Do you happen to remember the specific date this happened and that you contacted Campus Police?"

"December 12th into the 13th. Officer Brogdon was who took the report."

"Would you be willing to sign a release to allow me to get your medical records? Just for the rape kit information?"

"I guess so."

"What hospital did you go to for the exam?"

Jenna shot Jaxson a look. "If you need a break, Darcie, I understand. We can follow up by phone."

Her voice sounded shriller this time. "Let's just finish up. I can't remember for sure. Maybe St. Francis."

"Do you or your parents have a copy of that protective order you filed for?"

"No, my parents gave all of the paperwork to Devon's dad when we signed the agreement."

"I'm sorry for intruding so much. That should be enough to corroborate your story and help corroborate Claire's accounts of what Devon was like."

Jenna walked across the room and covered her hand with both of hers. "Thank you so much for your help. We'll get out of your hair and let you have the rest of your weekend."

Chapter 21

Once they were back inside Jaxson's BMW, he exclaimed, "If that guy weren't already dead, I would kill him. What a jackass! No excuse for attacking women."

"Glad to know you feel so strongly about it. You believed her then?"

"Yeah, if you watched her, it was like she was actually remembering and reliving it as she was telling it. I think she'll be a helpful witness for you and support Claire's experience with Devon. I think you need to go into a more detailed interview with Claire about their sex life. He didn't force himself on one partner and magically stop being abusive. Maybe we can get her to describe a typical good day and a typical bad day."

"I like that."

"Aren't you glad you came along on this trip? I don't know that she would have been as comfortable just talking to me about that personal of an issue."

"Yes, I was impressed with her. I hate that it happened to her, but I'm sure she is really helping other women out there."

They rode along with country music playing in the background as she started reading the latest Danielle Steele novel to break up the pace from the thrillers. When she looked up, they were crossing the Red River back into Oklahoma. "We're making quick time I see."

"Not too much traffic going back this way. Did you want to stop somewhere to eat?"

"Maybe a little something or stop at a gas station and get a candy bar and fresh drink."

"I'm pretty sure there's a gas station and fast-food combo coming up soon."

"Perfect."

****

He drove into her driveway, and he pulled her luggage out for her. "I can bring that in for you."

"Thanks, I'd appreciate it." She walked to unlock the front door, and he brought the luggage into the foyer. They stared at each other for a moment. "Stay," she blurted out.

He raised an eyebrow in a silent question. She stammered, "I meant you can stay for dinner. I'll order something in. I plan on just relaxing and watching movies, if you want to join."

He smiled at her obvious nervousness and awkward attempt at flirting. "Sorry, but I have to pick up my dog from my brother's, and I promised him I would hang out with him tonight."

"What kind of dog do you have?"

"Rottweiler. His name is Blitz. I thought you were a cat person?"

"I love my Midnight, but I like dogs too. Do you have a picture?"

He unlocked his phone. His wallpaper was Blitz posing with a toy in his mouth. Then, one on his back with his legs in the air. He played a video of the dog running as fast as he can around his backyard. "He's beautiful."

"He's all boy—not beautiful—but he is a good-looking dog and an awesome companion. You'll have to meet him one day."

"Is he friendly?"

"With dogs, it's all about the owners and how you raise them. He's a lover unless you're trying to hurt me, or you are just a bad person in general."

They were standing mere inches apart, and another awkward silence followed. Finally, he broke it. "I better be going, but I'll see what you're up to tomorrow."

She nodded and moved to give him a hug. He was clearly surprised and tightened the hug but let her go and nodded at her and left. *What did you expect, Jenna? You've been keeping him at arm's length or insulting him since you met him.*

Chapter 22

The felony pre-trial docket was crowded like always. Jenna juggled ten clients that were in custody and tried to catch ADAs (assistant district attorneys) and make last-minute deals. Mary Ann, Blake, and Kirk were all on the docket today. "Kirk, let's work these out. We don't want to try these cases."

"You've had our offer. You have to convince me a real reason to change them."

"This guy, Johnson, you want seven years in prison for burglary. This guy is just a drug addict. Give him drug court."

"But he picked up three burglaries in the span of nine months."

"And he hasn't received any treatment."

"He was out of custody long enough in between that he could have sought treatment."

"You know how hard it is to get off meth. Now after six months of jail, he has sobered up and wants to get clean. I've found a place in Tulsa that has a bed for him. You can order him to report immediately and do thirty days inpatient and then come back and apply for drug court."

"I'll agree to let him apply for drug court, but no guarantees. A condition of bond will be immediate reporting to this rehab, and he will sign a release with the drug court team showing proof of his arrival and treatment. No second chances. He screws up in the application process for drug court, and it's straight to the pen."

"Fine. I'll write a court minute up and get him in line."

She served Mary Ann with her witness list and expert report for Claire's case. "Jenna, you're not actually going to try this thing, are you?"

"Yes, I am."

Mary Ann glanced down at the list, "Oh no. This Darcie isn't going to testify. I'll be filing a motion *in limine* on that. I'm not going to allow you to tarnish the memory of the real victim."

"File away, but his memory should be tarnished. He was a bad guy. You're on the wrong side of this one."

"I'll go for the max if she wants to play."

"Let's go."

She walked back to the defense table and called out, "Harry Reynolds." Her client was in custody and shuffled over to the defense table. "Harry, today is your lucky day. You've been in jail for six months, and the ADA is finally going to give you that deferred sentence. Let's go over this form."

"I get out today if I sign this?"

"Yes," she answered as she started filling out all the biographical information.

"And I won't have a record, right?"

"Correct."

Blake came over to her spot. "Jenna, why are you not pleading out this domestic abuse case today?"

"I'm not sure you can make your case. That's why. Have you read the victim's revised statement?"

"Jenna, now that's crap. You know they got back together, and he manipulated her into writing that."

"Maybe so, but I can't make him plead if he thinks he can beat it."

"How about setting it for a bench trial then?"

"I'll ask him. But if you drop it to a misdemeanor and give him a deferred maybe I can talk him into it."

"He has to take the fifty-two-week class though, and he's on notice that if I see another report, he's going to prison."

She signaled to her client Riley to come forward. "Hey, so I've talked the ADA into reducing the charge to a misdemeanor and giving you a deferred sentence with the yearlong class but with a warning, if he sees you back, he will send you to prison."

"But if she doesn't testify, can't I beat it?"

"Maybe, but they can play that 911 call, which I will tell you is powerful and terrifying. Neither a jury nor a judge will like it. They can also introduce her medical records and pictures. You can take that risk, but I don't recommend it."

"Ok, fine. Let's just get this over with."

The judge called Claire's case, and they moved forward. Claire whispered, "Do I have to say anything?"

"No, just agree."

"I understand this case is ready for trial. Do we anticipate any pre-trial motions?"

Mary Ann blurted, "Yes, Your Honor, I plan on filing motions *in limine*. I would ask that you set a special motion hearing so we can resolve those issues for trial."

"Ok, motion hearing and final pre-trial is scheduled

for August 20th at 9:00 A.M. This trial will be first up starting on August 31st."

As Claire walked back to her seat, Jenna told her about Darcie and that she would be back out to see her soon. Claire sighed. "Look. Lara is here."

"Don't let her bother you. Darcie hated her too." That made Claire smile.

****

Claire watched the rest of the docket proceed, enjoying being out of the jail cell, but seeing Lara reminded her of a vacation she took with Devon and his parents before she was pregnant. His parents rented a resort on Myrtle Beach in South Carolina. The place was three stories high and right on the white, sandy beach. She and Lara went shopping while Devon and his dad golfed. She bought a couple negligees, a bustier, and a corset thinking she would surprise Devon. When he got back, she hadn't put everything up yet, he saw the lingerie and flipped out yelling, "Who are you buying these for?"

"For you, of course. I thought it would be fun on our vacation to spice things up." She trembled, and her heart pounded as she saw the look on his face.

"Our sex life isn't good enough for you as it is?"

"No, I didn't mean it that way. It was a surprise for you. I thought you would like it."

"I didn't marry a whore, and those look like you are about to walk the streets looking for a man. Take them back tomorrow. Do you understand?"

"Yes, of course, I'm sorry."

"Who have you been screwing?"

"No one. I've only ever been with you." He backhanded her, and she fell backward and hit her head on the corner of the dresser. She cried out in pain and touched her head and felt the blood dripping from the wound.

"Damnit. Look what you made me do! I'll go get ice." He left the room presumably to go downstairs to the kitchen when Lara came in and saw the blood.

Lara walked into the attached bathroom and brought back a bandage and placed it on her head. "You know your job as a wife is to build him up and make him feel secure—not have him question whether or not you are being faithful."

"All I did was buy lingerie. Why does he have to lose his temper like that? Can't you talk to him?"

"He's my son, and I love him. The fact that you can't handle him is not my problem. I told you way back that you wouldn't fit into this family and what was needed to fit into this family, but you didn't listen."

Devon came back and paused in the doorway. "Mom. It was an accident."

"I'm sure, son. I'm headed to meet your father for dinner. She certainly can't come along in her current condition, but are you coming?"

"I think I'll stay and order us something in."

"Goodnight then. I expect to see you both for breakfast."

This many years later, and goosebumps still covered her arms thinking about the Ice Queen at that moment.

Chapter 23

Ashley played Go Fish with her counselor as she did every week. Payton then asked, "Ashley, you've been coming to me for a while. Your grandma says you have nightmares. Can you tell me about them?"

"I'm not supposed to talk about stuff like that."

"Who told you that?"

"Momma and Daddy."

The counselor gave her a puzzled look. "I mean before all this happened."

"This is a safe place. What you tell me is private unless you are in danger, or a judge tells me I have to say. It's ok."

"I have dreams about daddy hurting momma. Sometimes he was really mean."

"Are these just bad dreams, or did these really happen?"

Ashley drooped her head and wrapped her arms around her legs that she pulled up to her chest. "It really happened."

"When you say he was mean, how was he mean?"

"He would call her bad words and she would have bruises and stuff later."

Payton moved over and sat on the same couch as Ashley and touched her shoulder. "Ash, can you look at me?"

Ashley nodded, but pulled her legs closer to her.

"Did you ever see what caused the bruises on your mommy?"

"They always sent me to my room, so I wasn't supposed to. I would sit in the closet and put my hands over my ears and try not to listen, but I could still hear some of it. A couple of times I sneaked out to see. I saw him pushing her down and grabbing her. One time I saw him hit her in the face, and she had a black eye the next day. I watched her try to cover it with make-up."

"I'm sorry. Parents are supposed to keep you safe. I'm sorry you saw that. Was your daddy ever mean to you?"

"No. He called me his little princess and always brought me gifts." She moved to the table and started drawing. *I've already said too much. I wish she would just drop it already.*

"What would your mom do during these fights?"

"Sometimes she yelled back and other times I would just hear banging noises."

"How did that make you feel?"

"I don't know. Sad. Scared. I don't want to talk about this anymore." She threw the crayons down on the table.

"Let's talk about something else then. What kind of things did you do with your mom?"

Her face lit up, and she gave a toothy grin. "We played dress up; we played with dolls and decorated my dollhouse; we played games. She was the best cook ever. She made really good chocolate chip cookies!"

"That sounds fun. Did you ever help her in the kitchen?"

"Sometimes, I got to help make sandwiches or with the cookies."

"What about your dad? What did you and he do?"

"He taught me to play soccer and t-ball. He always was the coach for the team. I'm really fast!"

"So, did you play in a league with competitions and stuff?"

"Yeah, until he died. Nana doesn't think girls should play sports. She enrolled me in dance and tumbling."

"Do you like to dance, or would you rather play soccer?"

"I like soccer a lot. Dance is ok, but I like tumbling the best."

"Ok, Ashley, you know you are going to start seeing your other grandma on weekends. Are you excited?"

"Yes, because I only ever saw her on holidays or birthday parties."

Ashley walked out to the waiting room to her nana who was decked out in her newest Saks Fifth Avenue outfit and latest Louis Vuitton purse she had been droning on about. "Come along, Ashley, we need to run home for you to change before we go to the Club for family night." *That explains her over the fancy outfit.*

When they arrived at the club, about five families were already there including Lizzie and her stepmom. Samples of wine, cheese, and dessert trays surrounded the room. "May I go play with Lizzie and get a couple cookies?"

"That's fine. Just don't get into trouble."

Lizzie and she stocked up on chocolate chip cookies, cheese, crackers, and soda for them and settled in for bingo. "I'm going to win a prize this time!" Lizzie exclaimed.

"Me too!" The bingo caller started the game: G 53, I 30, B 4, etc. when a ringing phone caused her to look back and see her nana answer it. They continued playing until a boy about their age hollered, "Bingo!"

"Dang it!"

The second game had started when her nana sat back down next to Heather. "Heather, you're not going to believe this nonsense. That was the district attorney who just called me. He said that Claire's defense lawyer found Devon's old college girlfriend, who was crazy. Her lawyer has talked her into coming to testify about Devon and try to back Claire up that he was abusive."

"How can they defame the dead like that?"

"I don't know, but I'm getting my lawyer on this. I am the victim, not that witch who killed my son. The District Attorney assures me that he has one of his best trial attorneys on this case."

"Ugh, Lara, that's just terrible. You should go to the news. This just isn't right."

"Good idea. I'll get my lawyer on that!

"But even worse than that, the Court ordered me to send Ashley with Claire's mother every other weekend. I don't even know how that woman afforded an attorney. She lives in an apartment for heaven's sakes."

"Oh no! Does Ashley even want to see her?"

"She seemed fine when I told her, but I think she will be shocked after she spends a weekend with her."

****

"I wanna take Zeus to Grandma Khara's!"

"Ashley, he lives here."

"But he'll miss me."

"Yes, he will. This wasn't my idea for you to go stay there, so don't blame me. Talk to Khara about it."

110

"Are you going to take care of him while I'm gone?"

"Yes, Ashley." Nana nodded and tapped her watch. "Hurry and get your bag in here. I need to talk to you.

"I don't know what may happen over at Khara's, so I'm giving you a cell phone in case you need to call me. I programmed my number in as well as Heather's and Lizzie's. I will monitor your phone usage, so don't get on social media. You can download games and text Lizzie, but nothing else or I will turn the internet off."

"Cool! Thanks."

The doorbell rang then. "Time to go." Her nana answered the door, "Khara."

"Lara. Is Ashley ready?" They glared at each other.

She peeked around her nana. "Yes, Grandma Khara, I'm all packed."

"Wonderful, let's go."

****

Ashley hadn't been to Grandma Khara's in a while. She lived in an apartment on the second floor with a balcony overlooking the pool. "Can I go swimming?"

"Sure. Did you bring a swimsuit?"

Her face fell. "No, I didn't know I would need one."

"That's ok, honey, we can buy one later."

"Have you talked to Momma?"

"Yes. I've talked to her and gotten to see her twice. She loves and misses you very much. She was so excited to get your letter. Did Lara let you send that?"

"No, a friend of mine helped me. How is she?"

"She is doing the best she can. How about we write her again?"

"Do you have crayons? I want to draw her a

111

picture."

"Yes, and we'll take pictures of you to send her too!"

Chapter 24

Jenna's phone rang, and she jumped, but answered when she saw it was Jaxson. "Hey stranger."

"Turn on channel 5 now!"

She did so. "Oh no!" Lara and her attorney were talking about how Claire Brown, who murdered her son, was defaming him from the grave. Lara stated through tears, "They say he abused his wife and are bringing an old college girlfriend, who spent time in a mental hospital to destroy his legacy and reputation." At the end, Lara looked directly at the camera and declared, "I will use any legal measures necessary to get justice for my son."

"Why is this news that they are covering now prior to the trial?"

"She's poisoning the jury pool. This is outrageous. Let me put you on hold right quick." She dialed Mary Ann who finally answered on the third ring. "Did you know about this?"

"I'm off the clock. What are you talking about?"

"Turn to channel 5 and maybe you'll catch the end. Lara Brown is poisoning the jury pool by saying that Claire and our witnesses are defaming the memory of her son and she will do anything to protect his memory."

"I didn't know anything about this. Your girl is guilty as sin, but I fight my battles in the courtroom and not in the press."

"You better not have put her up to that or I will be filing misconduct charges against you. I intend on filing for a gag order first thing Monday morning!"

"I didn't know, Jenna. I'll see if I can get ahold of the full interview to see what all was said." With that, Mary Ann hung up.

She switched back to Jaxson, "You still here?"

"Yeah. What did she say?"

"She claimed she didn't know anything about it. She doesn't typically play to the press, but sometimes her boss does. I wonder if he knew. Lara and her late husband were big contributors to his campaign. I know what I will be drafting this weekend."

"Is that all you're doing this weekend?"

"I don't have much planned. You?"

"I'm singing with the band at a gig this weekend. You want to come?"

"Where are you singing?"

"Place on campus corner. You should come hang out."

"I might just do that."

"I'll send you the details. Later."

****

"Ms. Miller, are you with us?" Judge Carpenter quipped.

"Yes, Your Honor, I'm sorry. My client is ready to change his plea of not guilty to guilty pursuant to the plea paperwork presented."

"Mr. Thornton, have you signed these papers?"

"Yes, Judge."

"What are you pleading guilty to?"

"Second felony driving under the influence."

"What do you understand your sentence is going to be?"

"Five years suspended."

The docket continued for what seemed like forever, and her imagination was running wild. Jaxson and his band were so good. *Every girl in the place wanted him, but I can't really tell if he is into me or not. I mean he hasn't even tried to kiss me even though there have been moments.*

"Ok, so what gives?" Amanda asked as they walked back to the office.

"What do you mean?"

"You've been distracted all day, which is not like you. So, who's the guy?"

"How do you know it's a guy?"

"Trust me, I know that look. It's a guy. Plus, we've been friends for the seven years you've worked here, and you've never had that look. So, am I right?"

"Yes, but I'm not sure what's going to come of it. I'm being one of those girls we hate and overanalyzing everything trying to figure out if he likes me or not."

"Just have fun and let him know you like him. You're so reserved; I've never seen you flirt."

"Because I'm terrible at it. You're right though. I just haven't even tried this in so long. Plus, I'm not sure I'm in his league."

"You're a lawyer, how could you be out of his league?"

"Because he's gorgeous and I'm just, you know, me." She pointed to her body.

"First of all, you are prettier than you give yourself credit for and, if you put more effort into it, you'd be surprised how many heads you would turn. Do you have a pic of him?"

"Actually, we took a selfie."

She showed her the picture. "I can see why you are distracted. He is hot. Good job, girl."

"He is, isn't he? That's why I'm afraid he's maybe just into the chase or a player because he could get any girl he wants."

"That's pretty stereotypical and judgmental. Not all of us are that way. Just give it time, and don't be like me and sleep with him from day one." Only Amanda could get away with saying that in a way that didn't make you hate her.

"Don't worry. We are nowhere near that. It's been a decade since I've even kissed a guy."

"You need to rectify that situation as soon as possible. Go out and live a little."

****

She sat at her dining room table thinking about what excuse she could use to text Jaxson when her phone rang. She didn't want to talk to anyone, so she silenced her phone, but then it started vibrating again and again. She saw it was an unknown number and normally wouldn't answer but they were so insistent that she worried there might be an emergency.

"Hello?" All that she heard in the background was a quick whoosh as if the person was trying to calm themself. "Hello? Are you there?" She waited a little while, and the breathing became louder and heavier. She hung up and the phone vibrated again and again. The third time it rang she answered again, "Hello?"

"You chose the wrong side." The menacing voice sent a chill down her spine.

"What?" But before she even finished the word,

three beeps echoed in her ear, and they were gone.

Chose the wrong side? Wrong side of what? Could it be this case? I didn't really choose it though. It was assigned. But what else could it be?

She hurried to the keypad to turn the alarm on. Suddenly she didn't feel secure in her own home.

Just to be careful, she retrieved her baby Glock 9mm out of its safe, loaded it, double checked that the safety was on, and put it in her nightstand by her bed.

You're overreacting. It could have been a wrong number or someone playing a joke. And even if it was for her, it wasn't exactly a threat. But she was on the wrong side before…when that innocent baby died. The memory of the mother in those pictures seared in her mind. Blood ran down her face and dripped down her shirt. Her left eye was swollen shut. Flaming red marks lined her cheeks. Her nose curved to the right. Agitated fingerprints circled her biceps. *And it was my fault. I helped him get away with it, and my cross-examination and closing arguments helped manipulate her into taking him back.*

Chapter 25

"State of Oklahoma v. Claire Brown. State present by Mary Ann Steele. Defendant present in person and by her attorney Jenna Miller. First, we need to address the most recently filed defense motion regarding pre-trial publicity and possible juror contamination.

"While Lara Brown, as the mother of the deceased, certainly has a right to be heard under Marsy's Law to be informed of all court proceedings and to be allowed to speak at any possible sentencing hearing; however, I will not make legal decisions based on news coverage of this trial. I also expect to be able to find twelve impartial and unbiased witnesses in less than two weeks.

"I am issuing a gag order on all attorneys and witnesses in this case until after this trial is over. Now, let's move on to the State's Motion *in limine* regarding Defendant's Witness Darcie Johnson. State, it's your motion," Judge Henson announced in his no-nonsense way.

"Your Honor, the Defense wants to assassinate the character of the victim who is not here to defend himself. Not only is their defense to claim without any evidence that she was a battered wife, but now bring an old girlfriend to testify to an alleged assault that he was never charged with."

"Ms. Miller, is there anything to corroborate Darcie

Johnson's testimony?"

"Yes, Your Honor, we have a copy of a non-disclosure agreement that Ms. Johnson and the deceased signed about the assault, which is why no charges were filed. We also have a copy of a SANE exam she took after the rape and the findings support her story.

"In addition, Your Honor, our defense is self-defense or battered woman syndrome. The character of the victim in this case is absolutely relevant to this case! If it hurts his reputation, that's incidental. Ms. Brown is facing life in prison, and not allowing her to put on a full defense could be reversible error."

"Let me see these exhibits that you have." She brought them forward. The judge then asked, "State, you have copies of these, correct?"

"Yes, Your Honor, but we do not believe these corroborate her story. It is circumstantial at best."

"I'm going to take this under advisement and rule before we start trial on Monday. Be here at 8:30."

Claire whispered, "Is that good or bad?"

"It just means that he is going to look at the law and rule, but the law is on our side."

"Hey, I don't know if this is helpful or not, but I've been journaling, and this is kind of a history of our relationship."

"Thank you. It will help me prepare for trial."

****

About 6:30, she left the office and saw that someone cracked her Cadillac SUV's windshield and slashed her tires. Under the windshield wipers, she saw a note. Without thinking about evidence, she grabbed it and saw it said, "This is your last warning, stop it now."

Stop what? She looked around and saw no one. Her hands were shaking which made it difficult to dial 911.

"What's your emergency?"

She paced back and forth in the parking garage. "I'm in the parking garage across from the courthouse and someone vandalized my car and threatened me."

"Can you tell me your name and what floor you're on? Someone will be dispatched now."

"Jenna Miller, I'm one of the public defenders. I'm on the 4th floor near the elevator."

"Someone should be arriving any minute. Do you want me to stay on the line with you?"

"No, that's okay."

She dialed Jaxson's number and he answered on the first ring. "Hey how did the pre-trial go today?"

"Jaxson," her voice cracked.

"What's wrong?"

"The officer just got here. Hold on."

"Officer? What happened? Where are you?"

"Parking garage."

"Jenna, what happened? Are you ok?"

"Yeah, I'm fine, but my car is all messed up. Hang on."

"Ms. Miller, are you all right?" the officer asked.

"Just shaken up. I'm physically ok. I walked out to my car and found it like this."

"Do you have any idea who would have done this?"

"Only thing I can think of is that someone doesn't like that I'm defending Claire Brown. Trial starts next week."

"No angry ex-boyfriend?"

"No, I keep to myself."

The officer took pictures and placed the note in an evidence bag. "You know how this works. I need you to fill out this statement. I'm calling in a detective, and we will see what we can find out."

"I have received a few strange phone calls."

"What do you mean strange?"

"Unknown calls multiple times a day. When I've answered usually, they just breathe on the other end. The last one I answered, he said 'You've been warned.' "

"He? Do you know who it is?"

"No, I didn't recognize the voice, but it was deep and almost sounded like they were disguising their voice."

She was finishing up her written statement for the officer when Jaxson ran up. "Jenna, are you okay?"

"I'm fine, really. I just need a ride." Despite the situation, she couldn't help but smile that he rushed over when it wasn't even clear what they were doing.

"Officer, can I take her home?"

"Yes, a detective will follow up with you soon, but we will need to process your car tonight before we release it to you."

As they walked toward Jaxson's car, she told him about everything including the phone calls.

"Why didn't you tell me about the calls?"

"Why would I? I didn't think anything about them until now."

"Maybe because I'm a private investigator. Maybe because I can run traces and forensics on your phone. Maybe because I thought we were friends."

"I didn't tell anyone about it until today."

"Do you have any idea who is making the calls or

would have done that to your car?"

"Has to be someone on the opposite side of a case. The Brown case is the only high-profile case I have right now."

"Then, you're in danger until this trial is over."

"Probably just trying to scare me or shift my focus away from this case. That's not gonna happen. Hey, you drove past Enterprise."

"I know. No need for you to rent a car. You can use mine; I have my motorcycle."

"I can't ask you to do that."

"You didn't."

"I'm fine with getting a rental. You'll want your car."

"You're infuriating, you know that? Are you this way with everyone or just me?"

"What are you talking about?"

"Do you have friends? Real friends?"

"What is that supposed to mean?"

"Just what I asked. Do you let anyone close to you, or do you keep everyone at arm's length?"

She didn't answer at first, and the longer she didn't speak, the silence echoed through the car. "I have Amanda, but we're really more work friends. We don't do much outside of work. I'm a loner, and I'm used to taking care of myself and focusing on work."

"That's BS, and you know it. You're hiding from the world. Every time you and I connect, you push me away again. You're scared."

"Thanks, Dr. Freud."

"Am I wrong?"

She was saved from having to answer because they pulled into a driveway. "Is this your house?"

"Yes. What do you think?"

"Very nice. It fits you."

"Not sure if that's good or bad."

She followed him into the house and was impressed at how neat it was. A hundred-pound blur ran to jump on Jaxson. "That's my boy. We have company, so be easy with her."

She then saw his stunning Rottweiler in front of her. He walked around her and sniffed and then sat down in front of her and raised his paw. "He wants you to shake."

She bent down and petted him. "He's awesome." He handed her a set of car keys. "Thank you. It should only be a day or two to get mine fixed."

"I'm serious. You need to be careful. The threats may get worse. Do you have an alarm?"

"Yes, and I have my baby Glock."

"Do you know how to use it?"

"Of course, I know how to use it. I went through a class. I also practice once a month," she snapped.

"Sorry, but if you have a gun against an intruder and aren't comfortable using it, you can end up dead. I don't want that."

Her heart melted then. *What's wrong with me? Why can't I relax and flirt with him? Ok, here goes.* "It's not just you, and you are right about me. It's just easier keeping to myself. You don't get disappointed that way."

"You think I'm going to hurt you?"

"I don't know."

He walked over to her and touched her cheek and turned her face up to look at him. "I'm not a bad guy."

"I didn't say you were."

"Then, stop shutting me out." He moved closer and kissed her.

Chapter 26

Jenna opened Claire's journal and read an entry.

Today, he was mad at one of his colleagues—and not me for a change—he punched the wall, hitting a stud so hard that he broke a knuckle in his hand. I, of course, stayed by his side at the hospital and took care of him. He took me out that weekend, told me I was beautiful, and spent the whole weekend pampering me.

The storms came again. He told me that I was lucky to have him and that girls flirt with him all the time. I was speechless and so hurt, I wanted to leave, but then I would really lose him and couldn't handle that. He said, "You're just a three or a four and should be grateful that a guy like you loved me."

The entries became increasingly worse. She wasn't a crier, but tears seeped out of her eyes as she finished the whole book. *If anyone qualifies for a battered woman's defense, it's her.* She valued human life, but the world was better off without him in it. Claire and Ashley were the real victims. When she started, the people she read about weren't real. *But I now know that what I do affects people's lives*. It was easy to take the abuser's side because she hadn't met his victim.

Legal ethics and rules sometimes conflicted with her beliefs. She just couldn't forgive herself. That baby's blood was on her hands. After she got him acquitted, he was more brazen than ever because he got away with it. The reports said he was punishing her for turning him in the last time and having to spend time in jail before the jury acquitted him.

A text came in from an unknown number. "You should watch your back." Then, a few seconds later another one, "You deserve to die and rot in hell."

Jenna took a screenshot of the texts and sent them to Jaxson. Within ten minutes, her doorbell rang. Jaxon barged in as soon as she opened the door.

"Give me your phone." He set up his call recorded number, blocked his number, and dialed the number on speaker.

It rang once, twice, three, four times until the voicemail clicked on. "You've reached 405-294-1234…"

He unblocked his number and tried the number again, with the same result. He called from her number without response. He texted, "Who is this? What do you want?"

Three dots appeared on the screen showing that the person read the message, but eventually they went away without a response.

"I really think you should have me stay here until this trial is over." Her eyes widened. She was not ready for that, but before she could protest, he said, "Don't worry. I meant in the guest room, but just so I can make sure you're safe. You could come stay with me if you would rather."

"I go to trial in two days. I need to stay focused on this case and not on this stuff. I don't want to leave my home."

"Fine, then let me stay here with you. This guy isn't stopping."

"You will distract me. Claire's life is in my hands. I need to win this case. It's my duty to make it right."

"What do you mean make it right?"

"Long story, and I don't want to get into it right now."

"You can't help Claire if you're dead."

"You're overreacting."

"And you are under-reacting!"

"Ugh, I shouldn't even have told you. I don't have time to argue with you. Investigate it if you want. Tell the detective or whatever you think you need to do, but I have to focus on this and practice my opening and make sure I haven't left anything out of my outlines."

"You're doing it again, Jenna."

"I don't have time for this! So please back off."

"Fine. Your wish is granted." He slammed the door as he left.

Why does everything have to be so difficult? Hopefully, he would get over it, but she couldn't be dealing with that kind of drama. Besides, nothing was going to happen to her. Someone was just trying to scare her. She could take care of herself.

Chapter 27

Jenna dressed in a power suit for her first day of trial: a perfectly tailored black suit with pencil skirt with black high heels. She entered the incredibly long security line to enter the courthouse behind many prospective jurors. She knew she had to be patient because the jurors would remember her, and it was important that they not hate her before she even started.

Claire wore a conservative white dress with flowers with subtle makeup that gave a glimpse of how she looked in her former life. Out of the jail scrubs, she had a young, sweet, and innocent look about her. "Claire, how are you feeling?"

"Nervous, anxious, but ready at the same time." She fiddled with her fingers in her lap.

"Stay calm. It will take an hour or more to get the jurors checked in."

Jaxson texted, "I'm in the hallway. You want my help setting up?"

"Claire, I need to set up in the courtroom." She walked outside and found Jaxson in the hallway. "Thanks for the help. Let's go down to my office to get it."

"You're welcome." He had been cold toward her since the other night, but he hadn't completely blown her off, so she thought there might be a little hope for them.

The adrenaline pumped inside her, and she could hardly keep still. "You ok?"

"I just hate the waiting. I'm ready to get started, and I don't even get to speak to the jury for a while because the State always takes forever with their *voir dire* questions."

"You're over prepared and will be fine. Besides, you have the best trial record around."

"How do you know that?"

"I do my research."

She smiled and touched his hand. "Thanks." He tensed and moved away to open the door to the courtroom. *I should have just let him stay, but this distraction is exactly why not. We have only kissed once, and already half of me is worrying about him instead of my case. Once we start, I'll be in the zone.*

When Claire and she entered the courtroom, the potential jurors were already in the pews. Mary Ann and Blake followed behind her. Mary Ann sniped at her, "Last chance before your client gets life in prison without parole."

"We'll take our chances." Claire looked frightened. Jenna whispered to her, "Remember what we talked about. The jury is watching you even now. Don't look worried because they may think you are acting guilty." Claire nodded and sat beside her.

The Court Clerk began calling out the names of the first twenty-two jurors. Jaxson was plugging the names of all those jurors into an app that would scan all their social media and court records quickly. This technology was invaluable, and Jaxson's agreeing to enter the information for her was a lifesaver. She sprung for this herself because the public defender's office did not have the money for those luxuries.

Mary Ann droned on about elements and that they don't have to prove motive or what time of day it happened because those are just details. Mary Ann started planting seeds of doubt about any domestic violence.

A prosecutor of all people should understand the cycle of violence and how the situations only deteriorate until the end. Jaxson slipped her a note that one of the jurors had three protective orders out against him and one dismissed domestic abuse charge, and that one of the female jurors used to work for the YWCA.

Yes, if I can only keep her on the jury, but if not, I can at least use her to educate. One wife of a police officer rattled on about how sometimes the victims have attacked her husband, so she had limited sympathy. She's got to go.

The former YWCA juror spoke up. "It takes an average of seven times for a woman to leave her abuser, and many times, women do not report. Domestic violence is not that clear cut as women just walking out the door."

Nice. Someone other than me made that point.

Mary Ann pounced. "Ma'am, have you been a victim of domestic violence?"

"No, but I worked with survivors of domestic abuse for five years at the YWCA."

"Do you really think that you can be fair and impartial about a case where a woman is claiming domestic violence?"

"I do. I would listen to all of the testimony and evidence."

"Are you more likely to agree with someone that

claims to be a domestic violence victim?"

"I am sympathetic to victims of domestic violence, but I will be fair and listen to the evidence. A number of people do falsely report domestic violence for one reason or another."

"So, in your time at the YWCA you did deal with women that falsely claimed domestic violence?"

"It was rare, but yes sometimes in divorce or custody situations."

"How would you determine who was telling the truth or not?"

"In that job, we accepted everyone at their word, but you can get a feeling if someone is lying or being genuine. Sometimes in the way they describe the abuse."

When Mary Ann made her point, she asked if anyone had ever been falsely accused of anything. One juror raised his hand and said he was once charged with embezzlement, but it was proven that someone else in the company framed him. *Interesting that the juror with the domestic violence history is not saying anything.*

Finally, about 1 PM, when Mary Ann finished her questioning, Judge Henson gave them an hour for lunch. Jaxson and she went over their notes from the morning in a cafe across the street from the courthouse. They ate lunch, but things were still tense between them, and he was all business. *Couldn't we be somewhere in between hot and cold?*

Every lawyer's handwritten *voir dire* sheet looked the same showing all the seats with the jurors' names and scribbles all over the page. The app's results were organized, readable, and enlightening. They discussed each one and mostly agreed on who she had to get off that jury for Claire to have a chance.

I'm so glad he is helping me. Doing this alone is painful and one of the reasons I like having a second chair if I can. "I would like Claire's perspective, but the jailer took her back to jail for lunch since she can't feed her because of some stupid jail rule."

"She's probably too overwhelmed to have an opinion, but just ask her what her thoughts are before you begin."

"I will. Thanks again for helping with this."

"No problem."

"Jax, don't be mad at me, please. Let's talk after I get through this trial."

He just nodded. "We better get back."

Chapter 28

"I promise my version will go quicker than the State's because she has covered a lot already." The jurors smiled and nodded. She had to cover reasonable doubt, self-defense, and battered woman's syndrome with the jury.

Her first question was to juror number 8 with the protective orders. "What do you think about the domestic violence laws?"

"I don't know. I've never really thought about it before."

"You didn't think about it when you were charged with it in 2017?"

"That was bullshit. Sorry, Judge, but I was falsely accused, and those charges were dropped."

"Isn't it true that those charges were dismissed because the victim did not show up to testify?"

"Because she knew she was lying."

"You mean that you two had reconciled by then?"

"Yeah."

"What about the three protective orders against you?"

"Two of those were dismissed too."

"Sir, do you really believe that you can be fair and impartial in a case where our defense is about my client being a battered woman?"

"Yeah, I can be fair."

"Are you more or less likely to believe my client because of your experiences?"

"I don't know. She's charged for a reason, and a lot of women lie to get something out of it."

"Judge, I ask that he be excused for cause."

Judge Henson looked to the State. "Do you have an objection for the record?"

Mary Ann jumped up, "Judge, may I *voir dire* the witness on this specific issue?"

"Go ahead."

"Sir, you have not ever been convicted of any kind of domestic violence crime, correct?"

"No, ma'am. I don't hit women."

"Then, you were falsely accused?"

"Yes, I was."

"But you aren't saying that everyone accused of domestic violence is innocent, are you?"

"No, of course not."

"So, can you promise to follow the instructions of the judge and hold off on making a judgment until after you heard both my and the Defendant's case?"

"Yes, I can do that."

"Your Honor, he has said that he could be fair, so I would ask that he remain in the panel."

"Ms. Miller, I assume you want to respond."

"Yes, Your Honor, we have a juror that has been charged with domestic violence, has had three emergency protective orders against him, and one final protective order that is currently in effect. I don't see how we can expect a man who either has been perpetrating domestic violence or falsely accused of domestic violence to give my client a fair trial."

"I agree. Sir, you are free to go. Call the Court

Clerk to find out if you are needed for other trials." They restart a shortened process with the new juror.

She expounded on the presumption of innocence. "How many of you thought my client was innocent when you walked in the courtroom today?" No one raised his hand.

"Why? As she sits here, the State has not proven anything to you, so what would your verdict be?"

A juror in the back row spoke up. "Not guilty."

"Why do we have that rule, sir?"

"Because we don't want to wrongfully convict someone. The police need to investigate and prove that she committed a crime."

"Good. Now think to yourselves, are you the kind of juror you would want to decide your case if you were in her shoes?" After a pause, "If it were you seated at the defense table, what would you want to see and hear?"

She called out juror number two, who had barely spoken all day, "Ma'am, what would you want of a juror if it were you?"

"To really listen to the evidence and make sure that the prosecutor and police proved their case."

"Great answer. That leads me to the State's burden. I want to highlight a few things the State didn't tell you." She explained the different burdens of proof and why criminal cases require the State to prove their case beyond a reasonable doubt. She asked all of them to swear that if the State did not prove beyond a reasonable doubt that her client committed a killing not in self-defense that they would return a verdict of not guilty.

She taught the jury about justifiable defenses to

homicides. She asked them questions about defending themselves or what they think they would do. The jurors all said they would fight for their lives.

When she finished, Judge called all counsel up to approach the bench to exercise their peremptory challenges. Both sides were able to remove five jurors. Once they chose their jury panel and picked an alternate, it was 4:30. Judge Henson excused them for the day with opening statements starting at 9:00 the next morning.

"What do you think about the jury?" Claire asked her.

"I think we have open-minded people, and that is always our hope. Get some sleep tonight because the big stuff starts tomorrow."

As the jailer led Claire away, Claire's mother approached her. "Ms. Miller, are you going to be able to get her out of here? I hate to say this, but now that Devon is gone, I can have my daughter back."

"Oh, Khara, nice to see you in person. Claire looks so much like you. I'm elated that you are here to support Claire, but I haven't decided if you will be a witness so you can't sit in the courtroom until you testify, or I release you as a witness."

"That's ok. I just want to be here. I feel helpless. How does it look?"

"We are early in this game, but I am going to do everything I can."

"Can you promise me she is going to come home?"

"Ma'am, I cannot promise or guarantee you anything. That is unethical and would be a lie. What I can tell you is I have prepared, she has a strong defense, and I will fight." Khara's face fell, but she nodded her head in understanding.

As Jaxson walked her to the car, she asked, "What do you think of the jury and how things have gone so far?"

"I think the jurors are already thinking about domestic violence and wondering whether she is a victim. No one horrible ended up on there."

Chapter 29

When Jenna walked into her office at 8:30 A.M., her assistant handed her a folder, "Hey, someone just dropped this off for you. I didn't know if it was for your trial or not."

She opened the envelope and saw pictures of her: several of her alone at home and a few with Jaxson and a note reading, "This is your last warning."

"Amy!"

Her assistant immediately returned, "What's wrong?" She showed her the pictures and note.

"Call Detective Meyers." She gave Amy his business card.

"You don't want me to just call the Sheriff's Office in this building?"

"He's already investigating this, but yes call them too, and see if we can get any surveillance footage of who dropped this off."

She then texted Jaxson. "You may be right. I received pictures of me at home with another threat."

Almost immediately he called her. "This is out of control."

"I know. Amy is calling Detective Meyers and the Sheriff's office. The pictures include you too."

"I'm not worried about myself."

"No, it seems like I am the only one worried about you."

"I'm walking in the door. I'm not letting you out of my sight until we figure out who is threatening you."

She saw him then. "Jax, I'm not completely helpless. I can take care of myself."

"This isn't up for debate." He held his hands up in a stop gesture that told her to let it go.

"Fine. I've got to get my mind in trial mode."

Deputy Vaughn strode into her office then. "Are you all right, Jenna?"

"Yes, I'm ok. I'm sure once this trial is over everything will calm down."

"Your assistant said that this isn't your first threat. I need you to start from the beginning."

"I can't do that right now. I'm expected in Judge Henson's courtroom in"—she looked down at her watch—"in five minutes."

"Call him."

"No, I have a client sitting in jail facing murder charges. I'm safe inside the courthouse anyway. I'll be fine."

When she arrived in Henson's courtroom, his bailiff Samantha came out and directed her into the judge's chambers. Mary Ann followed behind her as Judge Henson says, "So, Ms. Miller, I understand you have received a threat this morning. And not the first one?"

"Yes, Judge, but I'm fine. I think it is related to this case, but either way, I just want to get to work."

"Jenna, I understand, but you can't be fine. You need to finish filing a report and see if we can learn anything about who is threatening you. This could be grounds for an appeal if your mind is not on this case."

Mary Ann snarled. "Judge, I have witnesses here

139

and waiting to testify. I'll have one of our investigators assist the other officers working on this, but Ms. Miller is safer here in this courtroom than anywhere else. Let's not delay this trial. How do we know this isn't a tactic of the Defendant to delay her trial?"

"That's just ridiculous. My client has been in jail this whole time. If anything, she wanted to prove her innocence yesterday. I'm sure your people listen to her jail calls, read her mail, and toss her cell, so you know that's blatantly false."

"Enough!" Judge Henson interrupted. "I'm having the jury return at 1:30 P.M. Ms. Miller, take care of what you need to do. Ms. Steele, don't make unfounded accusations, and the Court would appreciate if your office gave this matter the attention it deserves and discover the culprit as soon as possible."

She sighed and reluctantly went into the courtroom and told Claire. "You're not backing off this case, are you?" Claire pleaded.

"Not at all. I want to get going now. I'm pumped and ready to go, but the Judge said no, so I will see you this afternoon. Everything will be fine."

When she returned to her office, not only was Deputy Vaughn there, but also Detective Meyers, and a D.A. Investigator Pierce. *I don't want to deal with this now. Just let me work, people!* "Let's get this over with."

"Jenna, this is serious. People who are brave enough to make this kind of threat in the courthouse are not playing around," Deputy Vaughn warned.

Detective Meyers jumped in. "We are dusting this for prints, but probably will not be helpful. They are pulling the surveillance videos. We should have the footage in just a few minutes."

Jaxson stalked in then and then introduced himself to the officers, and the four of them talked as if she weren't in the room. *I'm not a damsel in distress. This is getting irritating.* She drummed her fingers on her desk over and over; it took all of her self-control not to pace. She stood, planning to take her work to the conference room and practice her opening statement again.

"Where do you think you're going?" Jaxson barked.

"To the conference room. Calm down!"

He followed her. "Jenna, this is dangerous. Someone is stalking you, and it's escalating. First, he calls harassing you, then he vandalizes your car, then he sends threatening texts, and now he came to your office after taking pictures of you at your home! Do you have to actually be hurt to take this seriously?"

"I'm not stupid, but I have a job to do. I'm safer here than anywhere. Help them if you can, but let me work in the meantime. I will be fine if I can do my job and finish this trial. I'm trying to block it out and get through this."

"Jenna, you're not being rational."

"Jaxson, stop! I know of the danger. My heart is racing. My blood pressure is up. My breathing is shallow. I can't stop fidgeting. Will it take a full-blown panic attack for you to get off my back?"

"No, but you can't bury your head in the sand either."

"Jaxson! You need to leave now."

He moved closer to her. "Jen, come on. You don't have to handle this by yourself."

"If you want to help, find out who is doing it." She turned and sat with her back to him. *I know he's just trying to help and show he cares, but I don't want him to see me like this. We just started whatever this is. I don't want to depend on him. I don't even know how to do that.*

She practiced her opening, stopping and restarting every time she made any bobble. She always tried to deliver them without notes, but sometimes it just wasn't possible. She repeatedly reviewed her meticulous file to ensure that she had clean and highlighted copies of all reports and exhibits.

About an hour later, Jaxson, Det. Meyers, Dep. Vaughn, and Inv. Pierce walked in. Meyers stated, "Your secretary identified this guy as the one who dropped off the envelope. Do you recognize him?"

She looked at the grainy image and saw a man with a hat pulled down and glasses on. "You can't tell much from this."

Vaughn said, "Watch him walk in and back out."

She did and turned her head slightly to get a different angle, while rewinding and fast forwarding. "I don't recognize him, but something about him seems familiar."

"Is there any way these threats are not related to this case?" Pierce asked.

"I can't imagine who else would threaten me."

"Any ex-boyfriends mad that you are with Mr. Stone, here?" Meyers questioned.

She scowled at Jaxson. *I'm going to kill him for telling them that we are together. I wasn't even aware we were together, but I don't want my work life knowing about my private life.* "The last guy I dated was locked up in Vinita about a decade ago, so I don't think so."

"What was his name?"

"Erik Owens if you must know, but that has nothing to do with this."

"Why did he go to a mental hospital?" Vaughn probed.

"He shot his neighbor because he believed the neighbor was after me. He was a paranoid schizophrenic with schizoaffective disorder. I don't really care to continue this trip down memory lane. You can look up his report and case file in this county if you must, but please don't contact him. We haven't spoken in years, and I would rather not open that wound for either of us." Jaxson signaled to them to cut off that line of questioning, and for that she was grateful.

Pierce then piped in, "I'll get a copy of the D.A.'s case file." They finally left the room.

Jaxson gave her a quick hug. "I'm sorry. Come on, let's go to lunch."

"I thought I wasn't allowed to leave the building," she muttered.

"Jenna, I'm trying to protect you."

She saw her boss approaching. "Jenna, can I talk to you in my office?"

This is all I need on top of this day. This guy is under-qualified and overconfident in his job and only cares about himself.

"Jenna, what's going on? I thought the thing with the car was a one-time thing. Now, it has happened again. You have a murder trial this week. Do I need to assign someone else?"

"No, Derek, I have it under control. Nothing for

you to worry about it. Police are on it."

"I don't need this kind of publicity when the media already thinks we are on the wrong side of this. I just need to know your eye is on the ball. If this is a personal issue, you need to get that under control."

"Yes, I have every intention of winning this trial regardless of this nonsense. We live on the wrong side of cases."

"Fine, but you need to think about your future here if you don't win this case."

He's such a jerk. He's going to fire me if I lose this case. I'm making him look bad. Is he serious?

"Let's go." She beelined out of the office and over to the elevator.

"What's the rush?"

"I hate that guy."

"Your boss?"

"Yes, he's so pretentious and fake."

"You know you could go to any of the big firms or start your own firm?"

"Apparently, I will have to if I don't win this case."

Chapter 30

At 1:25, Judge Henson took the bench and signaled for the jury to enter. Mary Ann stood on behalf of the State and read the Information as required by law. She tried to appear interested, but this was routine, and she had read it many times. Then, the magic words started her opening, "To this the Defendant has entered a plea of not guilty placing at issue every element of this crime."

"Ladies and gentlemen, this is a case of greed and buyer's remorse. The Defendant met and married Devon Brown within a year of meeting. It was a whirlwind romance. Devon was a star athlete, academic all-star, and from a wealthy family. A couple years into the marriage, they had their daughter Ashley. The Defendant had it all. She didn't have to work. She lived in a large house and had everything she wanted, but somewhere along the way, this wasn't enough for her. She was tired of being a wife and a mother and wanted those partying years back that she missed as a new wife and mother. As the marriage between them deteriorated, she devised a plan to get rid of her problem—her husband. Once he died, she would receive a substantial life insurance policy, the house, and all the money he made during the marriage. She would be set. She could do what she wanted.

"The evidence will show that only three people

were in the home that night: The Defendant, the deceased, and their six-year-old daughter. The deceased was stabbed in the back. The six-year-old was asleep in her bedroom. Thankfully, she did not have to witness her father's slaughter. The Defendant was the only one with the opportunity to kill her husband. Devon Brown had no chance to react because the Defendant stabbed him in the back with the largest knife in their kitchen. He immediately went down and died within seconds. I suspect that the defense will argue that she was a battered woman and had no choice, but don't fall for it. It is shameful to assassinate the character of the murder victim when they have no chance to defend themselves. Ladies and gentlemen, you will notice that she never claimed to be this victim of abuse until after she killed her husband. At the end of this case, I will ask you to find her guilty and send her to prison for the rest of her life."

As soon as Mary Ann sat down. Judge Henson asked, "Ms. Miller, do you wish to make your opening statement now or reserve?"

"Now, Your Honor," she answered and moved toward the podium. "My life or his? That was the question that Claire Brown was faced with on the night in question. After years of physical, psychological, sexual, and financial abuse, she knew it was either her or him, and she fought back for the first time. As she struggled for breath against the kitchen counter, she grabbed the knife drying in the dish rack. She stabbed where she could reach, just hoping to disarm him. She didn't want to kill him. Despite the beatings, the manipulation, the threats, she still loved him. Also, along with the love was the terror the next assault would be her last and her six-year-old daughter Ashley would be left without a mother.

"Not only that, but she worried that if she were gone, Mr. Brown might take his rage out on their daughter. She fought to live for her daughter, who was asleep in her room. The State focused on the fact that she didn't report the abuse until after her husband was dead, but you will hear from experts that failure to report or cooperate is prevalent in situations of domestic violence. You will see bruises and injuries and hear about how they were inflicted. You will see medical reports of her injuries.

"You will even hear from a previous girlfriend of the deceased. She will tell you how the deceased viciously assaulted and raped her. I hope that you are never faced with the kind of decision that Claire was, but if you were, think about what you would do. At the end of this trial, I will ask you to return a verdict of not guilty and allow Claire to get back to doing what she does best—being a mother."

Blake took the first witness—the 911 operator—and after establishing who she was played the 911 call, which was played for this part. "I, I need help. My hu…husband."

"Ma'am, what happened to your husband?"

"He, he's bleeding."

"Why is he bleeding?"

Static noise followed by "stabbed."

"Are you hurt, ma'am?"

"No. Hurry, there's so much blood." The line went dead.

"Your witness," Blake said with a slight smirk to her that the jury couldn't see.

147

"No questions."

Next, Mary Ann called one of the paramedics to the scene to describe the condition of the deceased when she arrived. The paramedic testified that when she arrived Devon Brown did not have a pulse, was no longer breathing, and was no longer bleeding. Mary Ann then followed up with this question, "Did you examine the Defendant, Claire Brown?"

"No, I didn't."

"Did you speak with her?"

"Briefly yes."

"What did she tell you?"

"Not much. She seemed like she was in shock. She just said, 'I tried to stop the bleeding. I thought it would be worse to pull the knife out.' "

"What did you observe about her appearance?"

"That she had blood on her shirt and pants."

"Did you treat her for any injuries?"

"No, I did not."

"Did you notice any visible signs of injuries?"

"No, I asked her if the blood was hers, and she said no."

"If she had reported an assault, would you have assisted her?"

"I or my partner would have yes."

"Pass the witness, Your Honor."

The Judge nodded to Jenna, and she quickly walked to the podium. "Would it be fair to say that you were concerned about the man on the floor who had been stabbed?"

"That is why I was there, but I realized he was deceased pretty quickly."

"Had Mrs. Brown attempted to help her husband?"

"It appeared that she tried to stop the bleeding because there were towels on his back."

"Did you ask her what happened?"

"No."

"Why not?"

"Because if there was any chance of saving him, I had to attend to him right away. When I realized that he had passed, I didn't need to get more information from her. That's not my role."

"Do you remember what my client was wearing that night?"

"No, not particularly. I deal with a lot of people."

"I'm going to show you a picture and see if that refreshes your recollection. Are these the clothes she was wearing that night?'

"I believe so."

"She was wearing a heavy sweater and thick jeans and boots, isn't that correct?"

"Yes."

"In those clothes, would you have been able to observe many injuries?"

"Not necessarily."

"Thank you. Have you treated many victims of domestic violence?"

"Objection, beyond the scope," Mary Ann interjected.

"Defense, response?"

"Judge, the State used this witness as an expert in responding to emergency situations, and the question goes to that context."

"I'll allow it." He looked at the witness and said, "You can answer."

"Yes, I've responded to many domestic violence

scenes."

"Have you ever treated someone for strangulation when there were no visible signs?"

"Yes, it happens."

"But you still treat them for strangulation, correct?"

"If other symptoms are present, then yes."

"What are those other symptoms?"

"Broken blood vessels in the eyes, sometimes incontinence during the attack, blacking out, memory loss to name a few."

"Do you ever have victims of domestic violence refuse treatment?"

"Yes, it happens more than you might think."

"Nothing further, Your Honor."

Mary Ann stood, "Redirect?" Judge signaled for her to go ahead.

"Did the Defendant ever tell you that she had been strangled?"

"No."

"Did the Defendant tell you that she had been assaulted?"

"No."

"Thank you, Your Honor."

Judge Henson then said, "Let's take our afternoon break."

Claire grabbed Jenna's arm, "How do you think it's going?"

"Try not to stress. It's going as well as it can. I'll be back." She walked out with Jaxson for the break.

"Any news?"

"Not really. They said there were no usable fingerprints on the note, which we didn't expect anyway. You're doing good in there."

"We have a long way to go, but I didn't expect to make any headway with the paramedic, so that was a little bright spot."

Chapter 31

The prosecution's next witness was the detective who testified the same way he did at the preliminary hearing but added that he had further interviewed neighbors and friends of the Browns and none of them testified to witnessing or suspecting domestic violence.

"So, Detective, did you find a scintilla of evidence that the Defendant had been abused by her husband?"

"No, I didn't."

Mary Ann passed the witness and Jenna stood up and asked, "Detective, thank you for your service to our community. Did you interview my client's family?"

"No, I didn't."

"Did you interview the child?"

"No, she's only six and even your client said she was asleep at the time."

"Will you tell the jury what a forensic interview is?"

"It's an interview geared toward children or disabled adults?"

"Are you a forensic interviewer?"

"No, I'm not."

"But would I be correct in assuming that someone in your department is or you have a person that you use for those?"

"Yes, one of our other detectives is, and the child advocacy center has their own interviewers."

"But you didn't ask the child if there had been fighting between her parents?" She looks the jurors in the eyes as she asks this question.

"No, I didn't see the need."

"The child is in the custody of the deceased's mother, correct?"

"I believe so."

"Did she influence that decision in any way?"

"No. Why would she?"

"Would you agree that Lara Brown is an influential person in this community?"

"I don't know that I could say that."

"Are you aware that she is a long-time and major contributor to the district attorney's re-election campaigns?"

"Objection, relevance, and lack of personal knowledge."

"He can answer if he knows," Judge Henson responded.

"I have no idea who contributes to the district attorney—that has nothing to do with me."

"Did you talk to a neighbor named Larry Wilson?"

"I would have to refer to my notes. I don't remember everyone's name."

"He's an elderly man who has lived next door to them for a while, does that jog your memory?"

"Vaguely."

"Did he tell you that he thought the deceased was mean to his wife and that he once saw her with a black eye?"

"Absolutely not."

"Would you believe that is what he told my investigator in a recorded conversation?"

"I have no idea."

She made a showing of grabbing the recorder and looking toward the jury. "You are sticking to your story that no neighbors suspected anything?"

"It's not a story. It's true."

"Thank you, Detective, I'm going to show you some pictures of the scene and home and tell me if you recognize them."

"It's the Browns' home where Mr. Brown was murdered."

"Objection to the witness's use of the word 'murdered', that is the jury's determination," she jumped up and objected, mostly for the effect because jurors may think the witness is implying something he should not be.

"Let's stay with the words died," the judge admonished.

"I've marked these as Defense Exhibits 1-10. Are these fair and accurate representations of the marital home?"

"They appear to be."

"I offer Defense Exhibits 1-10."

"Admitted," Judge answered.

"Detective, I would like you to look at the door in Exhibit 1 and compare it to the other doors in the pictures. Notice anything?"

"It's different."

"Did you find that odd?"

"No, I didn't think about it at all."

"In Exhibit 2, do you notice anything about the wall?"

"No."

"You don't see the patchwork?"

"That could be anything."

"Objection, relevance," Mary Ann called out.

"What is the relevance, counselor?"

"The Detective indicated that he saw no signs of any disturbances or signs of domestic violence. I'm attempting to point out things he may have missed."

"Overruled."

"Look at Exhibits 3-5, what do you notice about the furniture in those pictures?"

"They have some marks on them. What of it? Again, I couldn't say what from."

She tilted her head and looked at the detective. "Wouldn't you agree that this house was exceptionally neat?"

"Appeared so."

"It didn't strike you as odd that in a house this pristine some furniture is ajar and damaged?" She turned her head to the side to the look at the jury to follow along with her point.

"No."

She shrugged. "Moving on, in Exhibits 6-7, in the master closet what do you see?"

"A hole in the wall."

"Doesn't that look like someone punched the wall?"

"Maybe, or someone fell into a wall or moving something hit the wall."

"Are you still sticking with the story of no evidence of violence in the home?"

"I have no evidence that the hole had anything to do with violence. I don't just assume."

"You don't assume. Hmm. That's good to know." She pinched her eyes together and shook her head.

"Counsel." The Judge admonished her. She moved on.

"Does there appear to be anything other than clothes in that closet?"

"Not from these pictures. I don't really remember."

"Did you get a search warrant for the house to search for evidence?"

"No."

"Isn't that common in a homicide case?"

"Not necessarily. We didn't need it when we knew who had stabbed him."

"Isn't it your duty to investigate and figure out why."

"I don't have to prove why."

"But didn't you state for the prosecutor you thought it could be for insurance money?"

"He was a rich guy and had a large life insurance."

"Did you look into other reasons? Like maybe he was beating her? Or was that too difficult?"

"Objection; compound question."

"Ms. Miller, you know better."

"I'll withdraw, Your Honor. Detective, did you attempt to figure out what was going on prior to the stabbing?"

"Yes."

"What did you conclude?"

"That he was in the kitchen getting something to eat and she stabbed him while his back was turned."

"Without any provocation just after several years of marriage, she walks in and stabs him in the back?"

The detective leaned forward in the witness chair, his body language stiff, and a scowl on his face. "It happens, lady."

Don't respond to that "lady" comment. Let it go!

"Ok sir, last question, look at exhibits 8-10. Tell the jury what is pictured."

"The flooring in the kitchen."

"Can you tell us what you see in Exhibit 10, the close-up shot?"

"Appears to be a small crack."

"Thank you. No further questions."

Chapter 32

Jenna packed up all her stuff, prepared to go home when Detective Meyers caught her. "Ms. Miller, do you have somewhere else you can stay until we catch this guy or things calm down?"

"Detective, I'm in the middle of a trial. I really don't want to worry about staying in unknown surroundings. I also have a cat."

"I can't make you do anything, but this is against my advice. We can have patrol drive by your house more often, but they can't sit and guard you."

"I understand, Detective. Thank you."

"I know this isn't any of my business, but Mr. Stone is a former police officer and armed security officer and private investigator. I know he is willing to provide security for you. Let him stay with you. I didn't know him all that well, but he had a great reputation on the force."

She simply nodded. Unsure of what to say. She liked her private life to stay just that, but he was right. She walked into the lobby of her office and saw Jaxson waiting. "I thought you might have left."

"Not until you get to your car. This guy knows where you park."

"Thank you. I'm sorry about earlier. If your offer still stands, maybe it wouldn't hurt for you to stay in my guest room until this is over."

"I'd be happy to do so, and Jen, I'm not trying to make you uncomfortable. I just want you to be safe."

"I know. I don't like all this attention."

When they arrived in the parking lot, she saw that Jaxson was parked only a few cars away from her, and that made her smile. *It's amazing he's still around.*

"I'll follow you."

"Don't you need to go to your place to get clothes and hygiene products?"

"I've had a bag ready in my car for a few days in case you needed me."

She smiled, feeling touched. *Lighten up. You know you like him. What can it hurt?*

As they ate dinner that night, he asked, "Who do you think they will call next?"

"My guess would be the medical examiner or forensics. I would think they will put Lara on last. I think they will rest tomorrow, so we need to make sure Darcie is here tomorrow."

"How are you starting your case?"

"With the domestic violence expert to educate and explain that tests and surveys revealed Claire was a victim."

"Sounds like a strong opening. Then Darcie?"

"That is the plan. I would appreciate it if you would coordinate with her on where she's staying so we can practice her testimony."

"I can do that."

"What about Claire's family? Are you calling them?"

"I think maybe I will call her mom and sister briefly and end with Claire. We'll see how things go." She reviewed her outlines for her witnesses and added and subtracted things from each one. Law and Order SVU played in the background.

Jaxson stood up from the chair, "I think I'm going to take a shower before bed. I'll take you to the courthouse tomorrow if that's ok."

"That's fine. I want to be at the courthouse around 8."

"Not a problem. I'll be ready." He winked at her.

She walked over to him, wrapped her arms around his neck, and kissed him but pulled back quickly.

"That was a nice surprise since all I've seemed to do is get on your nerves lately." He didn't release her from his grip though.

She blushed. "I'm sorry. I don't like being pitied, and I'm not comfortable with people taking care of me."

"I'm not pitying you. I care. Do you not understand that?"

"You could have any girl you wanted. It's obvious anywhere we go. Why me?"

He pulled her tighter against him. "I enjoy being around you. You're beautiful, smart, quirky, and sweet, though you try to hide it, or at least with me, unless you really don't like me."

She laughed. "I do. You're just not the guy I thought you would be."

"Did I make a bad first impression?"

"I thought you were hot, but you seemed full of yourself."

"You were pretty icy that day."

He kissed her again. When they finally pulled away, they were both breathless. "So, are you going to be nice to me now?"

"Maybe." She turned and walked toward her bedroom.

He laughed. "I guess I can live with that. Sweet dreams."

Chapter 33

The next morning, Jenna came out of her room, dressed and ready at 7:30 A.M. She moved to her pantry to get a granola bar and something to drink when she saw Panera Bread. Jaxson sat on one of her barstools spreading cream cheese on a bagel. "How did you have time to get this?"

"Door Dash brought it. I realized I don't know your alarm code or have a key to lock it behind me."

"Thanks. That was thoughtful." As she ate an Asiago cheese bagel, she pulled out an extra key and handed it to him. "Alarm code is 1324."

"You look ready to take on the world, killer."

"I better be."

****

She settled into her place at the defense table when Claire came in. "What's going to happen today?"

"The State should rest their case today. Depending on time, we will either start our case today or tomorrow. Darcie comes into town today. Our expert is ready to testify, and we will start with her. I'm going to put your mom and maybe your sister on, and we will end with you. Don't worry, we will practice before then."

"Is Lara testifying today?"

"I believe so. I think the State will call the Medical Examiner first and then her. Just stay calm. Those witnesses will be rough on you, but we haven't started to tell our story, so don't panic."

Blake lingered in front of the defense table. "I see you have stayed on the case despite your little stalker. They figured out your fan yet?"

"I'm so grateful for your concern over my safety. Perhaps if you had better control over your witnesses, none of this would be happening."

"There's that paranoia again. I think you've spent too much time with your clients."

She pursed her lips, didn't bother looking at him, but waved him away. "Hate to remind you, Blake, I'm not the one who made this an issue, so you might tell Mrs. Brown that I don't scare that easily."

"I think you need to up your medication, Ms. Miller."

Before she could respond, Judge Henson came on the bench. "Anything we need to take up on the record before the jury comes in?" Both sides answered no. Then, the jury came in. "State, you may proceed."

"State calls Dr. Yarborough."

Mary Ann asked her all about her education, training, and years of experience. Then, she started into the meat of her testimony. "Were you able to determine a manner of death?"

"Yes, it was a homicide."

"How did you determine that?"

"I ruled out suicide immediately because of where the wound was located, he could not have stabbed himself. The likelihood of being accidentally stabbed in the back is so remote, it wasn't even a reasonable possibility."

"What about undetermined?"

"With the other information I have been provided that the Defendant's prints were on the knife and that she was the only other person there I had enough to conclude homicide."

"To be clear, what caused his death?"

"A stab wound to the back which penetrated his aorta."

"Was there just one stab wound?"

"Yes."

"How long would his death have taken after the stab wound?"

"No more than a few seconds because when the aorta is punctured, death is nearly instantaneous."

"As part of your investigation and examination, did you take pictures of the deceased?"

"Yes, both at the scene and in the morgue before and after the autopsy."

"I'm showing you State's Exhibits 6-15, do you recognize these?"

"Yes, these are the pictures of Mr. Brown I took on my autopsy table, which is a typical part of documentation."

"Your Honor, I offer these pictures and ask to publish to the jury."

"Any objection?"

"No."

Mary Ann took a few minutes going through each picture.

"Did he have any injuries consistent with an altercation before his death?"

"He had a few minor abrasions, but nothing that alarmed me."

"For the record, did anything in your autopsy or

investigation indicate that Mr. Brown was stabbed in the middle of a fight with his wife?"

"No."

"Nothing further."

The judge signaled her to proceed with her cross. She didn't see it as a text had come across her phone. "You've really done it this time."

Louder this time, "Counsel, any cross?"

"Sorry Judge." She hurried to the podium. "Doctor, can you explain what are the possible manners of death that you could assign."

"Homicide, suicide, accident, or undetermined."

"You can't know what transpired prior to his death, can you?"

"I can make deductions based on the evidence before me."

"But your deductions are educated guesses, at best?"

"They are based on years of training and experience and scientific evidence."

"I also would ask you to turn to State's Exhibit 9, one of the autopsy pictures, can you look at the deceased's right knee, what do you see?"

"There is a red abrasion."

"Couldn't that be a sign of a struggle?"

"It is certainly not enough to say that."

"But isn't it possible he received that abrasion from tackling someone and hitting the floor?"

"I would expect more of an injury from that."

"But it's possible."

"Yes, most everything is possible."

"You didn't examine Mrs. Brown, did you?"

"No, I didn't."

"If you had examined her and found a swollen face, bruises on her stomach and back, and red eyes, would that have changed your opinion on the manner of death?"

"Possibly, but I'm not going to speculate."

"Objection! Counsel is engaging in hypotheticals." Mary Ann snarled.

"She's an expert witness, Your Honor, and the hypotheticals have a purpose."

"I'll allow this up to a point, Counsel."

"Doctor, if you examined a body with a swollen cheek, bruises on stomach and back, and red eyes, what would you conclude?"

"That they had been assaulted and possibly strangled."

"Wouldn't part of your training and experience include examining bruise patterns to determine how they occurred?"

"Yes."

"I'm showing you what I've marked as Defense Exhibit No. 11, can you tell me what you see in this picture?"

"A bruise on a stomach."

"Can you determine how an injury like that occurred from this picture?"

"Completely out of context. that would be difficult."

"Objection!" Mary Ann shot up. "This is beyond the scope of direct."

"Your Honor, this is the State's expert witness who has stated that she ruled homicide because she ruled out other mechanisms of death. I should be able to explore her expertise as it relates directly to our defense."

"Allowed."

"Can you look at that bruise and tell the jury if anything stands out to you?"

"Appears to have an imprint that stands out."

"Could that imprint have come from this ring?"

"It's possible, but I definitely can't say that conclusively."

"What about this one on the back, what would you say about it?"

"I can't say a lot about it."

"Is that in a normal place that you would find an accidental bruise?"

"Not normally, but that doesn't mean it didn't come from an accident."

"Let me ask it this way. Could someone inflict an injury to themselves in that location?"

"Anything is possible, but unlikely."

"Doctor, what about this picture?"

"This one looks like fingerprint bruises likely caused from someone grabbing or squeezing, but again, out of context it would be difficult to say if it was some kind of assault."

"One more picture, Doctor. Can you say what would have caused this pattern of bruising?"

"It is hard to say definitively from a picture, but it could be from a belt."

"Doctor, I refer you to your report. You ran toxicology on the deceased's blood, did you not?"

"Yes, that is standard practice."

"Can you tell the jury what Mr. Brown's test showed?"

"Objection! Relevance." Mary Ann snapped.

"Counsel, approach."

"Your Honor, this is clearly an attempt to defame the deceased."

"Your Honor, whether or not the deceased had been drinking and taking drugs contributes directly to self-defense."

"What was in his system?"

"He had a blood alcohol of .10, opiates, and benzodiazepines."

"Judge, blood alcohol goes up after death and whether or not the deceased was taking pain pills is not relevant."

"If the combination affected his behavior, it is absolutely relevant."

"Step back." Then, Judge Henson directed the pathologist to answer.

"He had a blood alcohol content of .10 and presence of opiates and benzodiazepines."

"So, his blood alcohol content was over the legal limit?"

"Yes, but blood alcohol content tends to rise after death so that is not necessarily accurate."

"Is alcohol supposed to be taken with benzodiazepenes?"

"No. Usually the pharmacy places a label on the prescription."

"Can the mix of the drugs and alcohol affect behavior?

"It can. The mixtures can enhance the effects of the other substances and overdoses are more likely than just with taking one substance alone."

"Can it make a person aggressive?"

"Some anecdotal evidence suggests that but I'm unaware of specific medical research that says the mixture causes or increases aggression."

"According to your autopsy how big of a man was Devon Brown?"

"He was 6'4" and 240 pounds."

"Did he appear to be in good physical shape?"

"He did."

"Did he look like a former football player?"

"I could definitely see that. He was very muscular, and his body had the typical deterioration that one would expect from an athlete."

"What kind of old injuries did you see?"

"I saw damage to his knees, hips, and elbows, as well as previously broken fingers and knuckles."

"Let's talk about that broken knuckle. In your report, I noted that you indicated he had a broken middle finger and knuckle in his right hand. Isn't that sometimes called a boxer's fracture?"

"It is a nickname doctors use because of how common it is in boxers."

"Let me ask you, could one receive that kind of injury from punching a wall?"

"Yes, I could see that."

"Now, Doctor, if you had a woman on your autopsy table with fingerprint bruises, red eyes, bruises on back and arms, and a swollen slightly red cheek, what would you conclude?"

"Objection again, Your Honor, this is completely irrelevant and asks her to speculate in a hypothetical that has nothing to do with this case."

"Counsel, approach and stop the speaking objections!"

"Your Honor, she is an expert witness; she can speculate and engage in hypotheticals."

"But counsel, what is the relevance of a woman on an autopsy table with these injuries?"

"It would be our contention that Mrs. Brown had these injuries on that night, and no one bothered to document it. I'm asking the expert witness what she would conclude from those injuries."

"Strike the question and rephrase. Ms. Miller, you may resume."

"What would you conclude about a woman with a swollen cheek, fingerprint bruises, red eyes, bruises or red marks on various parts of her body?"

"That she had been involved in an altercation."

"Would you conclude that she had been assaulted? Possibly a victim of domestic violence?"

"Objection!"

"Disregard that last question. You may answer if you would conclude she had been assaulted."

"I couldn't conclude that just based on the bruises because I could not say who would have started such an altercation so would not conclude domestic violence."

"But those aren't typical accidental injuries, are they?"

"Not typical."

"Undoubtedly, not all at one time, right?"

"No, I wouldn't conclude they were accidental."

"Nothing further, Your Honor."

"Redirect?" Mary Ann pounced to the podium.

"Dr. Yarborough, would it be fair to say that you would never make a determination based on a picture or even a few pictures out of context?"

"Absolutely, I would not."

"Isn't it also possible that Mr. Brown received that red abrasion on his knee when he fell to the floor after being stabbed?"

"Yes, that is possible."

"Or that he ran into a kitchen island?"

"Yes, many things could cause that bruise."

"In your experience if a 6'4" 240-pound man, a former football player no less, were to hit a 5'4" woman weighing 110 pounds, would it leave documentable evidence."

"Generally, yes."

"Let me ask you this, if someone is strangled and causes the petechiae in the eyes that Ms. Miller was alluding to, would it be obvious to any medical professional?"

"If the strangulation was severe enough to cause petechiae, it is obvious and appears differently than just red eyes from allergies or drinking."

"So, the jury isn't confused, what are petechiae?"

"It is when blood vessels burst. During a strangulation if the neck is squeezed hard enough, the pressure can burst blood vessels in the eye causing the whole eye to look red."

"Nothing further, Your Honor."

"Ladies and gentlemen, we will conclude our morning testimony and resume after lunch."

Chapter 34

As Jenna and Jaxson exited the courtroom to head to lunch, Mary Ann was gesturing wildly at Blake at the end of the hall. "Your job as second chair is to make our case airtight. You should have seen those questions coming so we had more to combat that. You know what is riding on this case. No more mistakes!"

"Guess they are scared by your awesome cross. I didn't know you had any of that?"

"It came to me the other night. I love using their witnesses to make points in my case."

"Who else is listed on their witness list? I just have a feeling we haven't heard the worst."

"Let's look at lunch. I've talked to all of them, but I'll pull out my notes."

"She's called the 911, paramedic, detective, ME. I know they will call Lara, let me look at all these other names. Who is Abby Thomas?"

"She's a next-door neighbor."

"Did you talk to her?"

"Not really. She just said she didn't want to be involved."

"Ok. What about Nicole Brewer?"

"Devon's assistant. She just raved about what a great boss he was and couldn't imagine he would ever hurt anyone. Said he never lost his temper at work and that everyone loved him."

"The rest of these are other officers who responded to the scene or doctors that treated Claire from our medical records."

"I don't think Mary Ann would risk calling them, do you?"

"I wouldn't think so because it would give you more opportunity to talk about common domestic violence injuries. I can't see what you're missing."

"You have all of your recordings from your interviews handy right?"

"Of course, I put them all on CDs if you needed them."

She inhaled deeply and tried to keep the bile from rising in her throat.

****

When they returned from lunch, Lara took the stand. "Mrs. Brown, I know how difficult this must be for you, but can you tell us about your only son Devon?"

"He was exceptional at everything. He was a top athlete, top of his class, top in his firm in bringing in and keeping accounts. He took his father's firm and brought it into the 21st century. Outside of that, he was a loving husband and father. Ashley, who lives with me now, was the light of his life." Lara dabbed at her eyes with a tissue.

"How was his relationship with his wife Claire?"

"He was always head over heels for her from the beginning. I didn't think they were a good match, but there was no talking him out of it. They were inseparable, but I stopped seeing affection between them. He would tell me…"

Jenna popped up. "Objection. Hearsay."

"It goes to his state of mind."

"I'll allow it."

"Mrs. Brown, what did he tell you?"

"He said he was unhappy and felt unloved."

"What did you observe about the Defendant?"

Lara pointed at Claire. "She never seemed grateful for what she had. She didn't have to work, but she still wasn't happy."

"Let's get to that. You were just pointing. Can you go ahead and identify who your son was married to?"

"The Defendant Claire sitting at that table in a blue sailor dress."

"Thank you. Did you ever talk to Claire about their marriage?"

"I tried, and she just complained about all of the day-to-day things and that she didn't get to have a career. I kept telling her how fortunate she was to have everything she ever wanted. She still wasn't satisfied."

"Did your son ever abuse his wife?"

"No, of course not. They had their arguments like all couples."

"Can you think of any reason the Defendant would want to kill the deceased rather than seek a divorce if she was unhappy?"

"She signed a prenup that my late husband and I insisted on."

"What were the details?"

"If they divorced within ten years, each would keep their separate property. Devon's home, cars, and most of his assets were titled in the name of Devon's trust and were purchased with his own separate money from the trust. She would receive nothing other than her personal property or gifts received during the marriage and what the law requires as her share for what was earned during the marriage."

"What if he died?"

"She and any children would equally share the proceeds of his Trust."

"Can you estimate the value of his Trust assets?"

"About three million dollars currently."

"And if the parties divorced before ten years of marriage, the Defendant would receive none of that?"

"Correct."

"But if he died, what would she receive?"

"She would receive half and would manage their daughter's half until she was twenty-one."

"What about life insurance or retirement?"

"She was the beneficiary of those."

"How much did he have?"

"About 1.2 million dollars."

"Nothing further."

"Ms. Miller, you may cross."

"Mrs. Brown, your son also earned a good living during the marriage isn't that true?"

"He made about $200,000 a year when he died but worked up to that."

"In a divorce, she would still be entitled to her equitable division of income and assets earned during the marriage, correct?"

"Objection. Mrs. Brown is not an attorney."

"Your Honor, the State opened the door with these issues by speaking about what she would receive in the event of a divorce or death?"

"Objection overruled. Ma'am do you need the question repeated?"

"No, but I'm not an attorney. I thought the purpose

of his keeping his assets separate and the prenup was to avoid her receiving that, so I don't know. I can say he paid all of the bills with income, and was not the bulk of his assets."

"Are you aware that she was not on any of his bank accounts or credit cards?"

"Yes, he handled the finances."

"But don't you find it odd that they had no joint accounts?"

"It's not that uncommon, particularly because she had never been exposed to that kind of money."

"You mean she grew up poor?"

"Yes, she had no family money."

"Do you know how she paid for groceries, clothing, or daily necessities?"

"I believe she used his credit cards, or he gave her cash."

"You mean an allowance?"

"I don't know that I would call it that, but he provided for her every need."

"Let me ask you this, if the Defendant wanted a divorce, how would she be able to retain a lawyer?"

"I don't understand what you mean."

"If everything was in his name, how could she pay a lawyer without his knowing?"

"I don't know what money she had."

"Now you said your son never abused his wife. Do you remember when all of you went on a vacation several years ago and walked in on the Defendant's head bleeding?"

"Vaguely."

"Didn't she ask you for help?"

"No."

"Wasn't it obvious that your son had just assaulted her?"

"No, Devon said it was an accident. I had no reason to believe otherwise."

"You didn't question it either did you?"

"No, it wasn't my business."

She let that answer linger for a moment and stared at the jurors and shook her head as she said, "Wasn't your business, I see. Isn't it true the Defendant asked you for advice on Devon's temper and you told her to be a better wife?"

"I believe she was immature and wanted to party. She just needed to adjust to married life."

"That wasn't my question, did she ask you for help or not?"

"I don't remember what words she said, but they had been arguing."

"Were you aware Devon made her drop out of college and stay home?"

"They wanted to have a family and he had enough money. She was lucky to live the kind of life that she did."

"Do you know if that's what she wanted?"

"She did it, so I assumed she agreed to it. I never worked outside of the home. I told Claire that her job as a wife was to facilitate Devon's career and take care of the family."

"Isn't it true that Devon was the one that did the extravagant spending and not Claire?"

"He made the money, but I don't believe she turned it down or complained."

"Claire isn't the first woman to claim that your son assaulted her, is she?"

"That young woman was unstable."

"Was she unstable before or after your son viciously assaulted her?"

"Objection. Assumes facts not in evidence, irrelevant, and prejudicial."

"Watch it Ms. Miller. Mrs. Brown, you may respond."

"That never happened. He broke up with her because she cheated on him, and she retaliated. She spent time in a mental hospital after that."

"But your family paid her and her family to not pursue criminal charges or a protective order, isn't that true?"

"We weren't going to let her ruin our son's life."

"You all paid her family $750,000 isn't that correct?"

"Yes."

"You must have been concerned that people would believe your son raped her to pay that kind of money?"

"Just the accusation would have ruined his life."

"Yet you don't think it's possible that he could abuse a woman?"

"No, I don't."

"Nothing further."

Immediately upon my leaving the podium, Mary Ann stalked to the podium. "Mrs. Brown, are you aware if Claire ever filed a police report against Devon?"

"No, she didn't. At least not to my knowledge."

"How often did you see Claire?"

"Pretty regularly. I involved her in volunteering on the same committees as me."

"Did you ever see her with a black eye or bruises?"

"No, I didn't."

"Nothing further."

Chapter 35

"State, call your next witness."

"State calls Nicole Brewer." She heard the click of stiletto heels before she saw the tall, busty woman.

"Ms. Brewer, can you tell us about your relationship with the deceased?"

"I was his assistant," she answered in a honey voice that struck Jenna's last nerve.

"How long did you work for him?"

"About five years." She pushed a strand of hair behind her ear.

"Did you ever interact with his wife?"

"Yes, the firm had a lot of social events. They hosted parties at their house. She occasionally came into the office for them to go to lunch."

"What did you observe about their relationship?"

"It always seemed like they were very much in love. He had pictures of her and his daughter around his office. Pictures of them were his screensaver on his computer and phone. He adored her."

"When working for him, did you ever see Devon lose his temper?"

"No, men and women alike loved him."

"Ever see him act violent?"

"Oh no. I can't imagine that."

"Did you ever talk to the Defendant?"

"Yes, fairly often."

"Were you friends?"

"I would say acquaintances."

"Did you ever get the sense that she was being abused?"

"No. She was kind of quiet, but I envied her life."

"Can you think of any reason she might want her husband dead?"

"I'm ashamed to say this, but Devon and I had an affair. His heart always belonged to her, but we did sleep together off and on."

"Objection, may we approach?" Judge Henson motioned them forward. "Your Honor, this is the first I am hearing of this. The State didn't disclose this. She didn't tell this to my investigator. It was not in the State's summary of witness testimony. I ask for an immediate mistrial."

"State, what do you have to say for yourself?"

"Judge, she only just told us this information."

"When?" she hissed.

"Yesterday," Mary Ann answered with a smirk.

"Why didn't you tell the Defense?"

"She has been on our witness list for months. They had access to her. They had the same opportunity to learn this information."

"Why didn't you tell her once you learned?"

"It's not exculpatory, Judge. It actually goes to motive."

"State, I don't like this kind of game playing like this. I will allow it, but Ms. Miller, if you want time before cross-examination, I will allow it."

"I'd like a brief recess before my cross-examination to speak with my client and investigator."

"I'll grant that."

"State, you may continue."

When she sat back at the table, she furiously wrote a note to Jaxson. "What the hell? Didn't you interview her? Get her interview ready and find her statement to the detective." Then she scribbled to Claire, "What did I say about lying and hiding things from me?"

Mary Ann resumed her questioning. "Did the Defendant know about this?"

"I think she suspected it."

"Objection. Speculation," she snapped.

"Your Honor, if you will indulge, I believe her answer will show why she thinks this."

"Overruled."

"I accidentally answered his phone late one night. Our phones were identical, and I didn't even look. It was eleven o'clock. He told her we were working late to finish an important campaign, but I don't think she bought that. The next day he had me order her dozens of flowers and chocolates, and he told me he loved his wife. We didn't sleep together again after that, and she never came to the office again."

"When was this?"

"About a month before she killed him."

"Objection, move to strike the second half of that answer."

"So stricken."

Mary Ann smiled as she returned to her table. "Nothing further, Your Honor."

"Ladies and gentlemen, we are going to take our afternoon break. Please return to the jury room in thirty minutes."

****

When the jury left, she walked to the guard. "I

need to speak to my client in private."

"I can't leave you with her in this room, we can move to the room back there and close the door."

Her face was red, and her heart raced as she stalked to the conference room. When Jaxson and Claire entered the room, she exploded. "Why the hell did you not tell me about this?"

"I didn't think it was important, and I didn't know for sure. I just suspected. He never admitted his affairs. I wasn't upset, he would generally be in a better mood and not home as often, so he left me alone."

She slapped the table. "You didn't think it was important? The State just proved your motive to kill him! We've implied to the jury you didn't have a reason to kill him, but you did. Now you say this wasn't the only affair. Who else could they have in their back pocket?" Jaxson touched her arm, but she shrugged him off and paced.

"I'm sorry. He had an affair with the next-door neighbor after her husband died. I knew he was having an affair with someone else but wasn't sure who it was."

"Anything else you haven't bothered to tell me?"

"Not that I know of."

"Let me get specific. Did you have any affairs? Ever see a divorce lawyer? Tell anyone you wanted your husband dead?" Her pitch rose with every question.

"No. I didn't even have my own friends."

"Ever confront any of his mistresses?"

"Abby. She was always walking around outside in these skimpy bikinis and having pool parties and hitting on my husband…"

Jaxson interrupted, "Abby is the next-door neighbor, right? I would have researched these women had you told me."

"I'm sorry."

"And what did you say to her?"

"One day she was going on and on about how lucky I was to have such a charming and handsome husband. I told her the grass was always greener on the other side, and I would be happy if I were her."

"Jaxson, please look into both of these women and see if there is anything we can find that will help us, and quickly."

"If Abby talked to the D.A. and told them about this conversation, we may be dead in the water. You basically told her she should be happy her husband was dead. I don't even know if I can undo this damage." She turned her back and started to exit.

Claire called out. "Abby is remarried now; I doubt she would want to come forward now."

Jenna leaned over. "Let's hope not because that would not sound good to the jury."

****

"Ms. Miller, you may begin your cross."

She marched to the podium with a file and a recorder in hand. "Ms. Brewer, do you recall my investigator Jaxson Stone interviewing you?"

"I've talked to so many people. I don't remember."

"He's sitting behind defense counsel; do you recognize him?" She pointed to him.

She leaned over and eyed Jaxson. "Oh, the hot guy, I do remember him."

"Did you ever tell him you had an affair with your boss?"

"No, I didn't want to defame Devon. He was dead and I didn't see why it mattered."

"Ms. Brewer, look at this statement you made to the detective, did you mention anywhere about sleeping with the deceased?"

"No."

"When did you tell the district attorney this?"

"Yesterday."

"Isn't that convenient in the middle of a murder trial, you suddenly remembered you were having an affair with the deceased?"

"It was only after talking to the prosecutor that I realized that might be motive. I didn't want to lose my job at the firm."

"And why say something now?"

"I heard that she was claiming she killed him in self-defense, and I just knew that couldn't be true."

"Because you knew the deceased so well?"

"Actually, I did."

"Let me ask you this, when Claire regularly came into the office to see her husband, were you sleeping with her husband?"

"Yes, off and on. It was just a casual thing. She seemed more interested in their child than him. He just needed affection."

"You said you all socialized together, so every time you talked to her you were lying to her?"

"It wasn't a lie. I just didn't tell her."

"That would be a lie of omission, wouldn't it?"

"I guess."

"I'm going to show you pictures of the couple at firm parties. Do you recognize these?"

"Yes, I've seen these on Devon's rotating frame."

"What do you notice about Claire's outfits in all of these?"

She shrugged and raised her palm in a questioning gesture. "I don't know what you are getting at."

"Doesn't she have long sleeves or wraps on in each of these pictures?"

"So? I just thought that was her style."

"When she came in the office, did you ever think it was odd that she often wore sweaters, long sleeves, and jackets even in summer."

"No. She was skinny. I figured she was just cold-natured."

"Or maybe she was just covering up bruises?"

"Objection!"

"I'll withdraw the question."

"Did the deceased buy you gifts while you were having this affair?"

"Sometimes, yes."

"You said you envied Claire earlier. Didn't you mean, you resented her because she was married to the man you wanted to be with?"

"No. We weren't that serious."

"You didn't imagine being his wife and living in the big house with all of his money?"

"Everyone daydreams, so what?"

"Maybe you just hated Claire and that she took him away from you so all of sudden you decided to reveal that she might have been angry at him for an affair?"

"No, I just don't think she should get away with murder."

"You weren't mad that Devon broke up with you?"

"It wasn't that big of a deal. I knew he was married, and he wouldn't leave her. He was devoted to her even though he was unhappy because he didn't think she loved him anymore."

"So devoted that he was cheating on her?"

"Objection! Argumentative."

"Nothing further, Your Honor."

"State, anything further?"

"State rests, Your Honor."

"Ladies and gentlemen of the jury. The State has rested their case. We have a couple of things to take care of outside of your presence, and we will start again tomorrow at 9 A.M."

After the jury exited, Judge Henson looked at Ms. Miller. "I assume you have a motion."

"Yes, Your Honor, I would demur to the evidence and ask for a directed verdict."

"That will be denied. Now do we know if the Defendant intends to testify?"

"Yes, Your Honor."

"Let's go ahead and make a record on that. Ms. Miller, call your client."

Judge Henson swore Claire in, and she sat in the witness chair. "Ms. Brown, you understand that you and you alone have the right to decide if you want to testify in this case?"

"Yes."

"You understand that no one can make you testify and that if you testify you will be subject to cross-examination by the prosecution?"

"Yes, I do."

"Have you been threatened, coerced, or bribed in any way to testify in this case?"

"Are you under the influence of drugs or alcohol today?"

"No."

"Have you been prescribed any medications that you are refusing to take?"

"No."

"Do you have any mental health disorders that would prevent you from understanding this decision?"

"No."

"Nothing further."

"Adjourned until tomorrow morning."

****

Ashley was playing Clue with Lizzie when she heard Nana's voice coming through the door. "Thanks so much for watching Ashley today. This day was terrible: that tramp assistant of Devon's testified to their affair. I know they are showing motive, but it's just all too much. Claire is going to testify though so can't wait for her to be destroyed."

Her face dropped and she whispered to Lizzie, "What's a tramp?"

"It's a bad name for a woman who sleeps around. I've heard my stepmom called that."

She looked confused. "I keep staying up all night to pray for Momma. I hate living with Nana."

Chapter 36

Jenna and Jaxson walked into Darcie's suite at the Hilton with a couple pizzas. "Thanks for bringing dinner over. I didn't really want to go out, at least not until after I testify."

"No problem. Thank you so much for being here. How are you feeling about tomorrow?"

"Nervous."

"The prosecutor will come after you hard. Lara already tried to plant the seed that you were troubled, so just don't let them get to you. Look at the jury when answering questions. Take a breath before answering, and if you are unsure about a question, just say so."

"Will Lara be in there?"

"Likely because she has already testified. She can't talk to you. Look at me, the prosecutor, or the jury and ignore everything else, unless the judge happens to speak to you."

"Ok. I had rape trauma syndrome and post-traumatic stress disorder is why I spent a month in-patient."

"I know, and you can explain that based on your experience and as a counselor. I am calling our domestic violence expert first so the jury should be educated on the dynamics of domestic violence."

"That's good."

"After her, you will be up. I would figure mid to

189

late morning. We can put you in a room, so you don't have to sit in the hallway and run into Lara. Jaxson will fetch you when it's time."

"Great. Can I meet Claire?"

"After you testify, absolutely. I know she would like to meet you, and she is grateful you are willing to tell your story."

As they walked out to the car, she beamed, "Let's go get Blitz!"

"What?"

"I feel bad for him being over there by himself. Bring him over to my place."

"I do miss him, and my brother and his husband are getting tired of walking him. If you're sure."

"As long as he doesn't hurt Midnight, I'd love to have him."

"He's a loving and obedient dog. He can stay outside in your backyard if they don't get along."

****

Jenna sat in her office with her eyes closed and her Air Pods in, listening to music to get her pumped up. She always did that to block out everything else in the world before crucial moments of her trials. Trials required laser focus because you had to be aware of everything that was going on: how the jury was reacting; what your client was doing; what the prosecutor was planning to ask; listening to your witness and making it flow like a conversation. You couldn't over-prepare your witnesses so it sounded rehearsed, but the jury must be able to follow the story.

I need get all the testimony out in a way that makes sense for the jury. She doesn't deserve life in prison. I should make that jury feel her terror, her fear, her feeling of helplessness. Hopefully through Darcie and Claire, the jury will realize what a monster Devon was. Her life is in your hands. So is little Ashley. Don't blow this.

She opened her eyes then, took out her Air Pods, emerged from the office, and bounced toward the courtroom. She was in her trial persona now: shoulders back, standing straight, smile on her face. She didn't feel like the geek or the bookworm in there. She loved the rush of adrenaline that flowed through her veins as she began the defense. "Defense calls Dr. Teresa Evans."

"Dr. Evans, would you tell the jury about your educational background?"

"I received my undergraduate degree in psychology from Oklahoma Baptist University Summa Cum Laude with Honors. Then, I earned my master's degree in marriage and family therapy from East Central University. Finally, I received my Ph. D from Texas A&M. During that time, I did thousands of supervised counseling hours to receive my licenses. Additionally, I continue to take continuing classes every year, as well as serve as an adjunct professor at the University of Oklahoma."

"Do you have an area that you consider your specialty?"

"I focus on helping adults and children overcome trauma from domestic violence and sexual assault."

"How long have you been working in this field?"

"In college, I first began working with victims of domestic violence and child abuse in several internship programs, so at this point I have worked with thousands of victims in the past twenty years."

"In your education and experience do you see typical patterns in these abusive intimate partner relationships?"

"Absolutely. I have a diagram that pictures the cycle of violence. Experts use two versions of this as either three or four steps. In my research and training, the cycle with four stages seems more accurate. The first step is tension building following by an incident of violence followed by reconciliation followed by a calm period. The reconciliation and calm phases are sometimes called the honeymoon period."

"Your Honor, can we publish this diagram to the jury?" The judge nodded. "What other things are similar in abusive relationships?"

"While every situation is unique to its facts as well as the client's reaction to it, in sessions I hear nearly identical descriptions of behaviors from controlling and manipulative behaviors to physical attacks to isolation. Additionally, the way the women describe their feelings inside those relationships is remarkably similar."

"Can you elaborate what you mean?"

"Yes, may I step down and show materials to better explain?"

Judge Henson nodded. She stepped down and pulled the top sheet off the easel and showed the domestic violence wheel. "I did not create this wheel, but this has been used in the field extensively and divides the day-to-day behavior of abusers in eight major categories outside of the actual episodes of physical or sexual violence."

"Can you explain to the jury about the power and control wheel?"

"Yes, society often thinks of domestic violence as

just episodes of a husband beating his wife, but it is much more than that. While there are various kinds of batterers, all utilize methods of power and control over their intimate partner. Looking at the wheel, he will often start with isolation or emotional abuse. Isolation often starts with what psychologists call 'enmeshment' or two people being joined all the time. It's the idea that you want to be together all of the time and that each other is all you need. At first glance, this sounds romantic and sweet, but what it does is slowly separate the victim from other people in her life. That is a necessary early step because if her friends and family see what is happening, they will call her attention to it and will interfere with his control and manipulation over her."

"It sounds like you are saying that domestic violence is more than just physical actions, but also psychological, is that correct?"

"Physical abuse is typically a corrective response when the partner steps out of line. If he has her under control with other tactics, the physical abuse may not be necessary. Batterers constantly minimize and deny any abuse while simultaneously breaking down their partner's self-worth to where they don't think they have other options. Victims often describe gaslighting that almost makes them question their own sanity."

"So, what happens to a victim that is subjected to this kind of power and control?"

"They feel helpless and anxious. They lose their identity. Their abuser almost takes on a Superman-like persona because the constant threats, aggression, and intimidation followed by attacks and overpowering of the victim which causes them to live in terror of this person. This terror leads to them irrationally believing anything they tell them. For example, many abusers use the threat of keeping their children away from them or not giving them a dime. The victim can't see that in seeking help the courts or other organizations could help prevent those things from happening."

"Is that why victims don't leave?"

"In part, yes, but also because they love their abusers as strange as that may sound. It may be a dysfunctional codependent kind of love, but they feel guilty about leaving them. Batterers also can and will be incredible romantic, charming, and sweet when they want to be. They use those good times to help their victims forget the bad times, which makes the victims hold out hope for those good times to return. Besides that, most victims are managing the danger in their own minds. They know if they attempt to leave and the abuser catches them, the beatings will be worse. Most batterers often threaten to kill their victims if they leave. It's like better to stay with the devil you know than the one you don't."

"Doctor, did you interview Claire Brown?"

"Yes, I conducted several psychological tests and conducted an extensive interview with her."

"What did you determine?"

"I would diagnose her with a generalized anxiety disorder, post-traumatic stress syndrome, and depression. I suspect the depression is more related to her present situation than an underlying mental health condition. I had no concerns about her having personality disorders or having sociopathic or psychopathic tendencies. I also believe that she was codependent with her late husband, which is likely a cause and effect of being a victim of domestic abuse."

"How did you determine that she was a domestic violence victim?"

"A number of things based on my training and experience dealing with victims. Part of it was in how she described the relationship. For example, when a stranger attacks someone, the victim will describe it with outrage and anger. A domestic violence victim will normalize it and talk about it with detachment."

"Can you explain what a codependent relationship is?"

"It means that one partner sacrifices their needs and wants in order to make the other happy. The other partner is typically a narcissist who insists on taking more power and control from the other. The codependent gives everything they can desperately seeking their partner's love and the relationship, while simultaneously sacrificing themselves, which ultimately leads to feelings of bitterness, resentment, and a total lack of self-worth and respect. A codependent person doesn't believe anyone loves them for them, but only for what they do for them, and so they try to do everything to make their loved ones happy."

"How does a codependent person handle an abusive relationship?"

"They are the most likely to become in that type of relationship because codependents are always seeking to please, fix, and take care of another person. Meanwhile, narcissists are always seeking to control their partner, and when the two meet, it's sometimes impossible to break that spell."

"Would a codependent person lie to protect their partner?"

"Absolutely. They believe that if they give undying loyalty and love to their partner, they will love them back and the situation will get better, but in reality the situation only deteriorates. As the codependents gives more and more to the narcissist, they lose their identity and realize that even though they have given everything, the narcissist still isn't satisfied."

"In your experiences with domestic violence victims, how common is it for them to not confide in others about the abuse?"

"It is exceedingly rare that a victim discloses while they are still in the relationship. In part because their abuser tends to become their universe, but also because they don't want to lose their partner. If they do discuss it with a close friend or family, they talk about it with rose colored glasses and never tell the whole story until significant separation or therapy."

"So, if Ms. Brown went to the doctor with injuries, would you find it unusual that she made up reasons other than abuse for how they happened?"

"No, not at all."

"No further questions, Your Honor."

****

"Ms. Steele, you may cross-examine the witness."

"Dr. Evans, these tests and surveys that you had the Defendant complete, they are based on her answers, isn't that true?"

"Yes, that is the accepted standard in the field whether an alleged victim or perpetrator. The test has questions built into it to measure truthfulness."

"Isn't it common for there to be police calls in situations of domestic violence even if the alleged victim doesn't pursue it?"

"It definitely happens, but not in all situations."

"You were hired by the Defendant to be their expert, isn't that correct?"

"Yes, but your office regularly retains me as well."

"How much did the defense pay you for your testimony?"

"I'm not paid for my testimony. I'm paid for my time. I bill at $100 an hour for my work."

"How many hours do you have into this case?"

She looked to the side counting hours in her head. "I haven't invoiced yet, but I believe I spent four hours conducting the tests and interview with Claire. I spent two hours reviewing and scoring the tests and my notes. Then, however long I am on the stand today."

"So, let's say about four hours today, then you will make about $1000 testifying for the Defendant?"

"That sounds about right."

"Do you think that the Defense would have used your services if you found that she wasn't a domestic violence victim?"

"I doubt that they would call me to testify, but I wouldn't jeopardize my professional integrity to earn a $1000. I have a very full practice. I'm in this business to help people, not pull something over on anyone."

"Let's talk about your findings and opinions. Would it change your mind about her being a victim of domestic violence if you realized that she stood to inherit a lot of money if her husband died?"

"That information would not change my opinion on whether or not I thought she had been a victim."

"Were you aware of that information?"

"I knew that they were wealthy. I didn't inquire about specifics because it wasn't relevant to my report."

"What about if you found out that she had recently discovered that her husband was cheating on her?"

"Abusive spouses often have affairs so that also wouldn't have much of an impact on my findings."

"You didn't have any concerns that these claims of abuse didn't surface until after she murdered her husband?"

"Objection!"

"Sustained. Watch it, Ms. Steele."

"I'll rephrase. Are you honestly telling this jury that you had no concerns that she didn't tell anyone about the abuse until after her husband was dead?"

"I view everything with skepticism, but in my interview, she seemed authentic. When she related the abuse to me, she was telling it as if she was remembering and reliving it. It didn't come across like she was reading from a script or making it up as she went."

"In your practice, have you ever known someone to claim abuse to gain an advantage?"

"Sure, I have had women come to me claiming that they were victims of violence or claiming that their children had been abused by their father. Even sometimes involving the children in that deception, but again I do not believe that is the case here."

"You are not infallible; couldn't it be true that the Defendant is a really good actress?"

"It would be complicated to fake all of the tests I gave her. These same tests police departments administer to ensure that mentally unstable people don't become police officers, but I suppose anything is possible."

"In your experience working with victims of

domestic violence, isn't it true that it would be much more common for the victim to end up dead rather than the alleged abuser?"

"Probably, but in those situations, adrenaline kicks in and people either fight, flee, or freeze. People do not always choose the same response. It's instinctual, not a conscious decision."

"Were you aware that the Defendant had no wounds or marks on her the night of the murder?"

"She told me about injuries that she had, and I know that I looked for pictures of her that night at the scene and there were none."

"Wouldn't you agree that you are more apt to believe that a woman was a victim of domestic abuse than a man?"

"It's far more common."

"But women do abuse men and murder their husbands?"

"Yes, it happens."

"Can you tell the jury what it means when a woman is referred to as a black widow?"

"That is not a psychological term, but I do know the term. It comes from the spider, and it's when a woman kills her mate after he has served his purpose."

"Nothing further, Your Honor."

"Any redirect, counsel?"

"No, Your Honor."

"Let's take our afternoon break. See everyone at 1:00 P.M."

Chapter 37

"The Defense calls Darcie Johnson." Darcie looked like a model as she walked to the stand in a navy blue sleeveless professional dress and stilettos. "Ms. Johnson, did you know the deceased Devon Brown?"

"Yes, he was my boyfriend freshman and first half of sophomore year."

"How did that relationship end?"

"Objection! Your Honor again for the record, I believe this testimony is irrelevant and prejudicial to the deceased who cannot defend himself."

"Overruled. Ma'am, you can answer."

"It ended after he raped and beat me for allegedly flirting with another guy."

"Can you tell us about your relationship prior to that?"

"I thought it was a typical college love story. Love at first sight. We were inseparable. That night we were at an end-of-the-semester party at his fraternity. We were all drinking a little bit, but Devon was drinking a lot. I thought we were all having a good time, laughing and dancing. Then he grabbed me by the arm and marched me into his room. I wasn't sure exactly why at the time."

"What happened when you got to your room?"

"As soon as the door closed, he slapped me so hard, I fell to the ground. Then, when I got up, he pushed me across the room where I fell into the wall. He was ranting about how I embarrassed and disrespected him by flirting with his friend. I had never seen him this angry before. He would get irritated from time to time, but nothing like this."

"What did you do?"

"I tried to apologize and explain that I wasn't flirting with anyone, but he held me back against the wall and started strangling me. I couldn't breathe. His eyes were cold and dark, almost inhuman. In a monotone voice, he let go and told me I needed to make it up to him and signaled and slightly pushed me to my knees. I knew what he wanted, and I had no idea how he would react if I said no."

"I know this is a sensitive subject, but what happened when you were on your knees?"

"He had me perform oral sex on him."

"What were you feeling in that moment?"

"Confused, scared, numb."

"What happened after that?"

"I'm not sure how to say this delicately, but that wasn't satisfying him quickly enough, so he pulled me up and threw me on the bed face down and forced himself inside me."

"Did you ask him to stop?"

"I screamed because he was actually ripping me open, but he covered my mouth and told me to shut up."

"What happened after that?"

"He forced me into the shower with him and then had me sleep with him in his bed. He slept like a baby and snored the whole night, but my heart raced all night, I couldn't sleep. I hurt and bled. I was terrified to even move. He finally let me dress and leave the next morning because I had to be out of my residence hall. I acted like everything was fine when I left."

"What did you do then?"

"I called campus security to make a report, but the officer wasn't taking it seriously, so I just went on home and told my mom. Then, I went to a hospital and had a rape kit. We called the police, made a report, and got an emergency protective order."

"What happened after that?"

"Devon's father called my parents and asked…"

"Objection. Hearsay!" Mary Ann interrupted her.

"Ms. Johnson don't repeat what other people said or told you."

"Without saying what someone said, what happened after the protective order?"

"Eventually Devon's parents and my parents came to an agreement that I would drop the protective order and not pursue anything, and, in turn, they would pay us a substantial amount of money."

"How did you feel about it?"

"I was not in any state to make any decisions. I didn't ever want to see him again, so I did whatever my parents thought was best."

"How did that experience affect you?"

"Objection, relevance."

"Judge, may we approach?" He motioned for them to approach.

"Judge, I know that the State will cross-examine her on her mental health, and it is only fair that we get to present that in direct."

"Ms. Steele, do you disagree?"

"Yes, Judge, I should be able to cross-examine her,

202

but going into all of her trauma isn't relevant for the limited purpose of her testimony of trying to prove that the deceased was abusive. How it personally affected her is not relevant to this trial which is about whether the Defendant murdered her husband."

"Limit your questions to mental health stemming from this incident."

"Ms. Johnson, did you have any mental health issues stemming from what you just told us about?"

"Yes, I had rape trauma syndrome and post-traumatic stress disorder. I spent a month in an inpatient facility handling that and stayed out of college until the next fall semester."

"Did you have any mental health issues or concerns prior to the attack you described?"

"No, I didn't."

"Are those conditions under control?"

"PTSD never totally goes away, but mine is managed and has been for several years now.

"Thank you. Pass the witness."

Mary Ann darted to the podium, "Ms. Johnson, so you admit you dropped out of college for several months and spent time in a psych ward?"

"I did after he raped and assaulted me."

"Your family got $750,000 out of your allegations?"

"The Browns paid us $750,000 to keep quiet about the fact that he raped and attacked me."

"Yes, in fact you signed a mutually binding non-disclosure agreement that you have now broken by testifying today and talking to defense counsel about this, isn't that true?"

"I checked with legal counsel, and the non-disclosure agreement was void when he died. I had kept my word until that time."

"Isn't it true that campus police didn't believe you that a crime had been committed?"

"The officer wasn't interested in hearing my story once he knew it was a fraternity party and we were drinking, and not to mention that Devon was a popular and wealthy football player."

"Aren't you aware that you as the victim don't actually have the right to decide whether or not to pursue charges, only the district attorney does?"

"I believe that I have heard that."

"So really your signing this agreement wouldn't have stopped the district attorney from filing charges and prosecuting him if they found the evidence convincing?"

"I don't know. I would assume it would be my word against his, and if I didn't say anything, it would just be his testimony. I think it would be difficult to make a case."

"Ms. Johnson, isn't it easy for you to accuse Mr. Brown of this now that he isn't here to defend himself?"

"Nothing about this is easy, Ma'am. I didn't want to come here and talk about the worst day of my life, but I felt like the jury would not get a clear picture of who Devon really was without hearing from me."

"Have you spoken to the Defendant?"

"No, I haven't."

"Did you know that the Defendant married Devon?"

"No, I blocked anyone that knew Devon. I moved to Dallas and have tried to think about him or that situation as little as possible."

"Isn't that a little convenient?"

"I don't think there was anything convenient about any of it."

"Would it be fair to say that you hate the Browns?"

"I don't know about hate, but I don't like them."

"In fact, you never liked his parents, did you?"

"I don't think that's fair. Lara made it clear that she didn't like me from the start. It seemed like the only people she did like was her son and husband. I was in love with Devon until that night. That further complicated healing from the trauma. Feelings don't just go away overnight. I missed the good times and still missed him even though I also hated him. It was only later that I realized that the relationship wasn't as glorified as I saw it at the time. Devon's dad was very distant and focused on his work."

"Would it be fair to say that you weren't sad when you learned of his death?"

"I didn't hear about it until the investigator called me, and it shocked me more than anything."

"Isn't it true that Devon no longer wanted to continue your relationship, and that's why you claimed he assaulted you?"

"No, it isn't. Devon kissed me and told me he loved me when I left, but he definitely was not wanting to end our relationship."

"So, we just have your word on this?"

"You could call my parents or look at the police report where we had to have him removed from my house. He was chasing after me, not the other way around."

"That would be a little self-serving, wouldn't it?"

"Objection."

"Withdrawn."

"Nothing further, Your Honor."

"Any redirect?"

"No, Your Honor."

"Let's call it a day and see everyone at 9:00 A.M. Remember do not watch the news or read any social media or newspaper accounts of this trial, and do not discuss this case with anyone until it is submitted to you for deliberations."

Darcie walked straight to Claire. "I'm so sorry I didn't want to fight and didn't stand up for myself and expose him. If I had, maybe you wouldn't be in this situation."

"It's not your fault. I should have left before it got to this point, but Devon did all of this. Had I never met Devon, I wouldn't have Ashley. Not you and me. I appreciate it more than you know that you testified here for me. You didn't know me and certainly didn't have to reveal all of this."

"I hope everything works out for you and you get your little girl back."

"Brown, we've got to go!" The guard hollered and led her away.

"Darcie, are you heading back this evening?"

"No, I'm going to spend a few days at my parents'. Please let me know the verdict. I'm going to get out of here though."

"Jen, are you ready?" Jaxson motioned to her.

"Not quite. I need to go down to my office and check in on things right quick before everyone leaves."

"Ok, I'm going to walk Darcie out to her car, so no one bothers her, and I'll be back up."

She nodded, trying to keep down the jealousy that was boiling in her. Darcie was gorgeous, and she just handled herself with grace. *I have no right to be. We aren't in a committed relationship. He can talk to or even date anyone else that he wants. She is about perfect. A much better fit than I am for him, but he's staying with me!!! He's the one that pursued me, and now that I'm really wanting to be with him, of course, he'll get interested in someone else.*

****

Jaxson called out to her as she was changing out of her work clothes, "I was going to make Italian for dinner, if that's ok with you?"

"You cook?"

"My mother required it. Do you care if I use your kitchen?"

"No, that actually sounds great. I didn't want to go out."

She appeared for dinner in a spaghetti strap top, shorter than her normal jean shorts, and flip flops. "Smells heavenly. What did you make?"

He turned to look at her and visibly swallowed, which made her smile. After a beat, he answered, "Spaghetti carbonara, garlic bread, tossed a Caesar salad, and some chocolate mousse."

"Wonderful. I'll set the table and put on soft jazz." She set out glasses, silverware, and pulled out her linen napkins. She also lit a few candles and dimmed the lights while trying not to be too obvious.

"You didn't have any wine, so iced tea is going to have to do."

"I'm sorry. I don't drink much, particularly not during a trial anyway."

"You killed it today. The jury was eating out of Darcie's hand, and your expert riveted them."

"Yes, I think it went well. Hopefully, her family further supports it, but a lot of it comes down to how well she does on the stand.

"So how was Darcie when she left?"

"She was relieved it was over, but I think still nervous for Claire."

"If you weren't on this mission to protect me, would you have gone out with her tonight?"

"What?"

"You two seemed like you wanted time to yourselves."

"Wait, are you jealous?"

"No, of course not."

"This is because I walked her to the car, isn't it?"

"She is gorgeous, smart, sweet, and seems to like you."

"She is all of those things."

"So why aren't you out with her tonight?"

He moved over to the chair closer to her and leaned his head on his palm and looked at her. "Are you trying to get me to go out with her?"

She averted her eyes. "You can do what you want. It's not like we are in a committed relationship or anything. I mean you are staying at my house and all, but it's not like I could be mad at you if you did."

"So, you're going to sit there and tell me it would not bother you at all if I called her up, or the court reporter that gave me her number today?"

"Kelli gave you her phone number? When did that happen?" *What? Women just walk up to him and given him their numbers? Why in the world would he stay faithful to me?*

"On one of the breaks, but calm down, I'm only attracted to complicated women who can't make up their mind on whether they like me or not."

"I am not complicated, and how do you know I can't make up my mind?"

"I wasn't talking about you." Her forehead scrunched up, and he laughed. "The look on your face was priceless." He moved over to the seat next to her. "So, you have made up your mind then? Mind telling me?"

She rolled her eyes. "You're impossible. Fine, yes, I was jealous and the thought of you with any of those women makes me crazy."

"Then, let's make this official. It's about time you be my girlfriend."

"Ok, but only if that dessert is any good."

He brought the dessert over then and fed her a piece. "Does that meet your approval?"

"It'll do." After a minute of enjoying the dessert, she stood and opened the back door letting Blitz in. "Let's take him for a walk." Blitz immediately started wiggling his butt.

"You want to walk him?"

"If we are going to do this, then he and I need to be good friends."

"Let's go, but I gotta warn you, he's more of a jogger than a walker."

"I'm up for the challenge."

****

Jaxson woke to a scream, and he ran into her room. "Jen, baby, wake up. You must be having a nightmare."

She flinched away from him, blinked her eyes a

few times trying to wake up. "I was having a nightmare. I was kidnapped and while I was gone, Claire was found guilty."

He stroked her back. "You're ok. I'm here with you. Nothing's going to happen."

She turned and held onto him. "I just have a bad feeling. Will you stay in here?"

"Sure, if you want." She scooted over so he could crawl in. He wrapped his arm around her and pulled her head against his shoulder. As he did so, he realized that he had been sleeping in boxer shorts only and she was in this skimpy short set, and as she rubbed on his chest, he couldn't help but respond. *Great, just when she was starting to trust me.*

She turned his head to kiss him, and soon he was lost in her and instinct took over, but he caught himself and pulled back breathless. "Baby, we better stop."

She was just as dazed and affected as he was. "Huh? Why?"

"Because this isn't the way for this to happen. I don't want you to have any regrets, and you need your sleep."

The crestfallen look on her face as she tried to move away from him felt like a knife to his heart. He stopped her from moving away. "No, you don't. I promised you that nothing would happen while I stayed here to keep you safe. I keep my promises, and that doesn't mean I don't want you, so I'm not leaving, you're staying in my arms, and going to sleep."

"Yes, sir," she mocked but settled back against him and relaxed.

Chapter 38

Jenna spoke with Khara outside the courtroom. "Are you ready? I just wanted to let you know why I'm just going to call you and then Claire: I like the momentum of how things are going. The jury wants to hear from her, and she is the key."

"She has a young baby and has barely been sleeping, so she was fine when you called and said you wanted just me and Claire."

"Remember, look at the jury when answering and don't let the prosecutor get to you. Don't get too emotional—either sad or angry."

"Got it."

"Jaxson will be out to get you as soon as we are ready."

"Before we bring out the jury, Ms. Miller, how many more witnesses do you have?"

"Two, Your Honor."

"I've reviewed the requested jury instructions and prepared a set. On our lunch break, I will provide a copy to each side and will review prior to the afternoon. I would like to be able to close and submit to the jury today if possible." The attorneys all nodded, and the jury proceeded in.

"Defense, call your next witness."

"Defense calls Khara Wilson to the stand."

"Ms. Wilson, what is your relationship to my

211

client?"

"She's my daughter."

"What was your relationship like with your daughter before college?"

"I was a single mom to her and her younger sister, and we were all very close."

"What about after she started college?"

"At first we talked almost every day, but within the first month, she met Devon and he monopolized her time."

"What was your impression of him?"

"Objection. Relevance."

"Overruled. You may answer."

"He was charming and polite on the surface, but something about him bothered me. He was so possessive of Claire. Once they got together, her world revolved around him. Once they were married, I saw less and less of her. She was rarely by herself. He always had to come along. If I called anytime other than when he was at work, I felt like she was always on speaker. I couldn't come over unannounced. Devon kept her on a tight leash. I basically only saw her on holidays and birthdays."

"What about when you became a grandmother?"

"It didn't get much better. I didn't even get to come to her birth. Devon called me after she was born."

"Did you ever see anything that caused you concern?"

"One time when I showed up unannounced, I saw ugly bruises on her arms. When she saw me looking, she put on a jacket or sweater. She made up an excuse for me to leave."

"Anything else?"

"The way that Devon talked to her was condescending and cruel, but he always did it in a way that tried to make people laugh. She acted like she was his servant, waiting on him hand and foot and trying to anticipate his every need."

"How would you say your relationship changed after she met Devon?"

"It severely deteriorated."

"Nothing further."

"Cross?"

"Briefly, Your Honor."

"Did you ever see Devon and your daughter fight?"

"No."

"Ever see him hit your daughter?"

"No."

"Ever call the police on him?"

"I called in a welfare check several months before he died, and she refused to take my calls or have any contact with me until she wrote me from jail."

"You mean several months before she murdered your son-in-law."

"Objection. Argumentative."

"Sustained."

"I'll rephrase. So, she quit talking to you after you called in a welfare check?"

"Yes."

"Did police contact you after that?"

"Yes, they told me she claimed to be fine and declined any help."

"Don't you think police would have investigated if they had seen something that caused them concern?"

"I assume so, but they said she wasn't cooperative."

"Did your daughter tell you why she stopped talking to you?"

"No, she just ignored me after that."

"You can only guess and assume why that was, correct?"

"I guess so."

"So, you have no proof of any wrongdoing on the part of the deceased, do you?"

"Seems fairly obvious from what I told you."

"But no videos, pictures, directly witnessing it?"

"I doubt most people beat their wives on video, so no I don't."

The judge announced, "Let's take a ten-minute break. I imagine the next witness will take a while."

Chapter 39

"The Defense calls the Defendant Claire Brown."

"Ms. Brown, can you tell the jury how you met your husband?"

"I was a freshman at the University of Oklahoma attending a party and he asked me to dance. At the time, I felt like Cinderella. He was charming and like out of a movie."

"When did you marry?"

"The next summer. He proposed in the following spring semester. He was graduating then and wanted to get married as soon as possible. It was romantic at the time getting attention from a star athlete on a national championship team. Not to mention, he was handsome, charming, and wealthy to boot."

"When did problems start?"

"Smaller problems were present early on, but I ignored them."

"What kind of problems?"

"He was controlling and possessive and demanded all of my time and attention. I didn't develop many friends because he wanted me with him all the time. He was my first love. I was ecstatic that he seemed so interested in me. I wasn't going to complain."

"When did the first major problem surface?"

"On the honeymoon, he threw me into a wall and threatened to hurt me if I ever laughed at another man's joke. Then, he went back to his loving, charming self. It was confusing, but after things rocked along well for a while."

"How did things progress from there?"

"I planned on attending college again that fall, but when it came time to go, he convinced me that he needed me to stay home for him. He would need me to entertain clients with him, and he wanted me available to come in for lunches and volunteer to help him build up his practice. I didn't want that, but I wanted to make him happy. His angry episodes came more often, and sometimes it was as if he despised me. Nothing I ever did was right or good enough for him. Things improved when I became pregnant with Ashley. He was thrilled, and most of the time during the pregnancy, he treated me like a queen."

"What about after you had Ashley?"

"It wasn't long before he was angry that I didn't keep myself up or have dinner or the house cleaned or any little thing. I think that was when he had his first affair."

"So, you knew about his affairs?"

"Yes, I suspected early on because he blatantly ignored me, and I would recognize that he wasn't obsessed with me, so another woman must be occupying his time."

"What do you mean by that?"

"He wouldn't touch me and often would stay in his office or a guest room. When he would get bored with the woman, then he would be wooing me again until he thought I was charmed and enamored with him again. The problem was I always loved him and was so desperate for him to love me, I did anything I could to make him happy. I made excuses for his behavior and gave up more and more of myself until I didn't even recognize myself anymore."

"You described angry episodes: can you tell the jury what exactly you mean by that?"

"Slapping, hitting, strangling, forcing sexual activity to make him happy. He always wanted to have sex after a major argument. It was a way of making sure he was still in control and that I wasn't leaving. He broke and hid sentimental presents of mine. He would pin me up against the wall and punch near my head. He would scream and belittle me for hours. I cried for a long time when he would do this, but he was so cold and almost seemed to enjoy it, so eventually I stopped crying or begging. I just walked on eggshells trying to avoid angering him."

"How was he with your daughter Ashley?"

"Like he used to be with me. He doted on her, took her for ice cream, and bought her anything she might have even wanted. He never hurt her and hardly even raised his voice."

"You said that he punched walls or destroyed property. I'm going to show you several pictures of your home, can you tell us if they are accurate pictures of your home?"

"Yes, this is my home."

"I'd offer these pictures as Defense Exhibits 13-17."

"Admitted without objection."

"Can you tell the jury what these pictures show?"

"In this first one, this is a hole in our master closet from where he punched the wall because he thought I was too friendly with a colleague we had over for dinner."

"Let's back up. To me that is a surprising event, yet you talk about it as if it were normal. Can you take us through what led to him punching the wall?"

"Things like this happened so often, it became normal. It was about six months before he died, we were entertaining people from his work like we often did. John, one of his associates, praised my cooking and told Devon how lucky he was to have me for a wife. Devon thought I had to have been sending him signals, but I wasn't. When they left, he started accusing me of having an affair. I denied it, ignored him, and walked to the bedroom. He followed me into the closet cornering me and demanding that I listen and respect him. I apologized and told him that he was the only man for me and that he should be mad at his friend if he was mad at anyone. He punched the wall right by my head and said, 'If you ever cheat on me, next time it will be your face.' " Claire flinched when she told of the punch to the wall.

She let that sit with the jury for a few seconds. "What about this door?"

"The door in this picture had to be replaced, and Lowe's had no more matching ones."

"Why did it have to be replaced?"

She bowed her head and blinked back tears. "I don't remember why we were arguing, but he had given me the silent treatment for almost two days. I went into his office to make up with him. He chased me out of his office and slammed his body against it with so much force it broke."

"What about this patched spot?"

She whispered, "He had to patch it after he threw

me into the wall."

"Can you tell the jury when that was and what was going on?"

"It was the night after I called Devon's phone and his assistant answered at 11 P.M. I knew his cover story was bogus. When he came home the next night, I was just so tired of it all. He brought me flowers and leaned in to kiss me. Normally, I would lavish affection on him and be excited, but I just didn't feel like faking it that day. It turned into a fight. He pushed me, I knocked over the nightstand, and my shoulder hit the wall." Claire grabbed a Kleenex, wiped at her eyes, and blew her nose.

"Ms. Brown, I know this is difficult, do you need a break or some water?"

"No, let's just keep going."

"Can you tell us about this box with knickknacks in it?"

"This picture shows a box of things of mine that he took from me: a charm bracelet my mom gave me, a picture of my best friend and me when we were younger, another picture of my mom, my sister and me that he ripped, the broken pin was from the sorority I was in, he also kept my social security card and birth certificate from me."

"Did you ever receive treatment for any injuries?"

"Yes, I went to the emergency room a couple times: once for broken ribs from when he punched me in the stomach and once for a broken wrist for when he yanked it too hard, but I lied and told the story he wanted me to tell. One of the pictures you showed the medical examiner was where he broke my ribs, but most of the time he managed his strength to hurt me just enough that it would not require medical attention."

"Why didn't you tell the doctors or nurses? They would have let you talk in private?"

"Because of Ashley. He always said he would make sure I wouldn't get custody and would end up on the street with nothing. I had nothing to call my own. Bank accounts and credit cards were in his name. He monitored any spending. I had nothing to fight him and nowhere to go. Besides that, I loved Ashley too much to risk it."

"You know now that divorce laws would protect you?"

"If you can get a lawyer to represent you for free maybe, but also, I loved him. I just wanted his anger under control. There were times that were idyllic followed by times of hell. I wanted him to look at me and love me the way that he used to. It was also embarrassing, and I didn't want anyone to know."

"I'm showing you what I've marked as Defense Exhibit 17, can you tell the jury what this is?"

Her eyes went down and the look of shame on her face was unmistakable. Then, she composed herself and looked up. "This is an apology letter Devon made me write him. It was something he periodically demanded."

"When did you write this?"

"I dated it October 21st of last year."

"Is this a letter you authored?"

"Yes."

"Would you read it for the jury?"

"Objection; hearsay."

"It's her words, Judge, not offered at all for the truth of the matter, but to show my client's state of mind in the marriage."

"Overruled, but you need to offer it as an Exhibit, first."

"Sorry, Judge, I offer Defense Exhibit 17."

"Admitted. Ms. Brown, you may read it now."

"Devon, I'm sorry that I'm such a disappointment to you. I'm sorry that I'm not devoted enough to you. I'm sorry that I have talked to other men when we have been out. I'm sorry that I'm so selfish and ask for more of your attention when you provide everything I need. I'm sorry that I am not as pretty as I was in college and don't keep myself attractive for you. I'm sorry that I caused you get upset and have to handle me. I will be better in the future. I know I don't deserve you. I love you and am sorry. Please forgive me. Your loving wife, Claire."

The Courtroom was dead still. That letter disturbed everyone. "Ms. Brown, why did you write that?"

"To show him I was sorry and hopefully calm him down. He would read from these apology letters later and remind me of what a bad wife I was."

"It sounds like you are apologizing for being beaten?"

"Essentially."

She stopped and made eye contact with the jurors letting this sink in. "You heard from his secretary that she never saw any injuries on you, can you explain that?"

"No one saw injuries on me other than Devon and Ashley, except for my mom and my neighbor Mr. Wilson because they surprised me."

"Why is that?"

"If I couldn't cover the injuries with make-up or long sleeves, I didn't leave the house. As you pointed out, in most pictures, I am wearing long sleeves or sweaters. If we had events to go to, he wouldn't hit me where it would show. I often had bruises on my arms or legs from his grabbing me or my falling down from his pushing me."

"Let's talk about the night he died. What happened?"

"We had entertained new clients of his. I thought the evening was fun, but Devon drank too much. The funny thing is, I thought he was happy and would want to make love and celebrate getting the new account, but shortly after they left, he grabbed me by the hair and dragged me to the kitchen screaming about what I made for dinner. He screamed, 'After all these years, you still belong in the trailer park!' That was one of his favorite insults. My mom raised me and my sister all by herself, and she did the best she could. We didn't have a lot, but we had everything we needed."

"What happened after that?"

"We started arguing. He slapped me to the ground. I could tell he was about to attack, so I tried to run, but he caught me and tackled me to the ground. I'm amazed that I didn't break anything, but I did have bruises on my back for a couple weeks after that."

"Is there anything of significance in this picture you identified earlier?"

"Yes, this crack in the tile happened that night when he tackled me to the ground. We never had any damage before that night."

"Did anyone take pictures of your injuries?"

"No. No one asked me if I had injuries. By the time you were appointed to represent me and we talked, most had faded."

"What happened after the tackle?"

"He picked me up and slammed me against the kitchen counter. I thought he was going to rape me then, but instead after he threw me there, I started to slide off and to the ground. He grabbed and pinned me to the opposite counter and started strangling me. I couldn't breathe. Part of this is fuzzy, but I remember struggling and grabbing for anything I could find. Then, he let go of my neck and fell to the ground. I realized that I had to have stabbed him and grabbed towels to stop the blood and called 911."

"The prosecution has seemed very concerned that he was stabbed in the back, can you explain that?"

"I will the best that I can. I didn't intend to stab him at all. I just wanted him to let go of my neck. I just knew if I didn't get him to let go, I was going to die. I kept seeing Ashley's face. I didn't want her to grow up without her mother, so I fought harder than I'd ever fought to get him off me. I was pinned against the counter so I could only try to hit him in the head or the back."

"Why was there a knife out?"

"I used it to cut vegetables and meat for the dinner I prepared. It was on the in dish rack on the counter drying."

"So just to be clear, why did you stab your husband?"

"To keep him from killing me."

"Nothing further, Your Honor." She smiled at her, trying to tell her to stay strong for the onslaught that was about to come.

"Before you start your cross, let's take a ten-minute break."

Jaxson walked up to her. "That went well. Are you feeling good?"

"So far so good," she smiled at him, thinking back to last night. "Go with me to get a drink."

He followed her and grabbed her hand as soon as they walked out of the courtroom. She no longer cared who knew. Besides, she liked the idea of the women in the courthouse being jealous of her.

Chapter 40

"Ms. Steele, you may begin your cross."

"Ms. Brown, isn't it true that your attorney was the first person you told about the abuse?"

"The first person I really shared all of it with, yes."

"Who else did you tell any of it to?"

"Ashley and I had to discuss it sometimes. I tried to shield her from it, but unfortunately, she saw and heard it sometimes. I also wrote to my mother from jail."

"You spoke to a child about these adult issues, isn't that selfish?"

"I didn't bring it up but sometimes she would ask me why her daddy was mean to me and why we fought. I tried to minimize it."

"So why didn't you have your daughter testify as a witness?"

"She just turned seven earlier this summer. No way I wanted her involved in a murder trial."

"But she is involved because you killed her father?"

"I guess so."

"Are you aware she has never told your mother-in-law about any abuse?"

"I'm sure she hasn't because it is my understanding that Lara doesn't allow her to talk about me."

"Wouldn't you be mad if someone killed your daughter?"

"Of course, but Lara knows what Devon was really like."

"So, isn't it possible it is just too painful for Mrs. Brown to think about her son?"

"It's possible."

"Now, if you were defending yourself, why didn't you tell the police that night?"

"I was in shock, and I was afraid no one would believe me. I wanted to get legal advice first."

"Isn't that convenient?"

"Objection!"

"Ms. Steele."

"You could have told doctors, nurses, or called police at any time, isn't that correct?"

"I promised him that I wouldn't tell when he took me to the doctor, and he stayed in the room with me."

"Your mother testified that she called in a welfare check on you and that you weren't cooperative with the police?"

"Of course not. When Devon realized that police were outside, he punched me in the stomach assuming I had called and threatened to kill me and Ashley if I said a word against him."

"Why did you stop talking to your mother then?"

"Because Devon said if I didn't, he would kill her."

"But yet no one else saw this side of him besides you and perhaps your daughter?"

"Most people don't beat their wives with an audience."

"But if you divorced your husband, you would only get a small portion of his money, isn't that true?"

"I don't exactly know what I would get, I never had access to his money."

"But you did know that he took out life insurance policies on both of you and your daughter?"

"Yes, that was his idea."

"If he died, you would inherit everything from him, correct?"

"I think Ashley and I would inherit, but I don't know the specifics. I wasn't really concerned."

"But weren't you? You said you had nothing without him and couldn't escape. What better way to escape than to kill him?"

"I don't think I escaped. I've been in jail for months and haven't seen my daughter since then."

"No one noticed any injuries to you that night, isn't that true?"

"No one really paid attention to me."

"What injuries should they have seen?"

"My face was swollen. My eyes were red. I had scratches on the back of my neck. I also had red marks that turned into bruises on my legs and back."

"You're also aware he had no marks on him?"

"I'm not surprised. He usually didn't."

"What hand did he strangle you with?"

"Both at one point."

"What did he typically wear on his right hand?"

"His national championship rings."

"Yet you didn't have ring indentions on your neck, did you?

"He also normally wore his wedding ring on his left, isn't that true?

"He was wearing both when he died, wasn't he?"

"Yes, I believe so."

"So, can you tell me, how you didn't have indentions on your neck if he was really strangling you to the point of not being able to breathe?"

She demonstrated his placing both hands around her neck showing his thumbs in the front and his fingers in the back underneath her hair. "I may have had indentions, but they would have been in the back underneath my hair. His hands were huge. He didn't need both hands to encircle my neck. Sometimes he used his right and other times both."

"Here's your book-in photo, can you point to any injuries on your face or neck for the jury?"

"You can't tell much from this picture, but you can see that my eyes are red."

"So, you claimed in your direct that you knew about his affairs, did they not bother you?"

"Of course, they bothered me, but he typically left me alone when he had a mistress, so sometimes it was easier on me to ignore it. Even when I did argue or complain, it didn't stop him."

"If he were such an abusive monster, don't you think he would have been abusive to his mistresses as well?"

"I don't know. He wasn't physically violent with me until our honeymoon."

"If you were really struggling for air, can you explain how you happened to grab a knife, not injure yourself, and stab him directly into his heart?"

"I don't know. I just know that I was trying to get him to let go of me."

"Pretty lucky shot, wasn't it?"

"Depends on how you look at it, I guess."

"Lucky for you. If you get away with this, you inherit his trust, the home, cars, and all bank accounts, isn't that correct?"

"I would assume Ashley and me. I haven't read his trust or his will."

"Your husband never told you?"

"He didn't think I needed to know about the finances. The only thing he told me was we need the life insurance in case something happened to him, so I could take care of our daughter."

"Let's look at these pictures of you and your husband. You're often holding hands or kissing or touching in every picture, yet you expect us to believe that you were a trapped, abused woman?"

"I loved my husband. I tried to make the best of everything. When we were in public, things were good, except when he made fun of me in front of others, but those would only be his close friends, who would assume he was joking."

"Did you regret getting married so young and not finishing college?"

"Sometimes, but Ashley made it worth it, and I wouldn't go back and change anything that would take Ashley away from me."

"How many times did you speak to Ms. Johnson prior to your coming up with the plan to murder your husband?"

"I'd never spoken to her until yesterday."

"So, you knew nothing about her allegations? Isn't that where you got the idea? She made allegations and got paid a large sum of money?"

"Objection; compound question and assumes facts not in evidence."

"Start with one at a time, Ms. Steele, and there isn't foundation for the question."

"You're telling this jury you had no idea about her

allegations?"

"I didn't even know her full name. All he told me was that his previous girlfriend was crazy and broke his heart."

"Isn't it true that you thought he was going to leave you for his mistress and that's why you killed him?"

"If that were true, I would have been free. I certainly wouldn't have killed him."

"You expect this jury to believe that you are completely innocent, stabbed a man in the back, and even though you had no injuries and would receive millions if you successfully get away with this battered woman's syndrome defense, that it's all just a coincidence."

"That's the truth."

"No further questions, Your Honor."

"Redirect, Your Honor." Judge Henson signaled for her to go ahead. "To be clear, did you plan to kill your husband?"

"No."

"Did you want your husband dead?"

"No, as crazy as it may be, I still miss him, but besides that, Ashley adored her father, and I wouldn't want to take her dad away."

"Did you hate your husband?"

"No. I was desperate for his love. I had to believe that he really did love me through it all. If I just tried a little harder. If I just loved him more. If I could just get things back to where it was 'us against the world.' I couldn't let go. It doesn't make sense. It was only until I had been in jail for a few months and realized that I was in less of a prison in jail than I was in my marriage that the magnitude of the abuse really sunk in."

"Did your husband ever tell you what would happen if you left him?"

"He said there was nowhere I could hide that he couldn't find me and if I left him, I would only see Ashley over his dead body."

"Thank you, Ms. Brown. No further questions. The Defense rests."

"Ladies and gentlemen, sorry we are late breaking for lunch today, but you can stay gone until 2 P.M. While we are getting close to the end, remember not to discuss this case with anyone including each other. You have not heard the closing arguments of counsel or received the law. Thank you."

"State, will you have any rebuttal?"

"Your Honor, may I have a few moments before answering that question?"

"Fine, counsel meet me in my chambers in ten minutes to receive the instructions and advise me about rebuttal, we will take argument if there are any objections to the instructions at 1:45."

"What does that mean?" Claire asks.

"The State is deciding whether or not to call another witness. She is worried the jury is with you. You did so well."

"Ms. Brown, we need to take you back for lunch. We'll have her back by about 1:45."

She walked back to chambers and saw Mary Ann and Blake. The bailiff gave them the instructions. "Blake will be calling another witness in rebuttal. Another woman came forward claiming that she was having an affair with Devon and that he bought her a promise ring. He told her that he planned to be rid of his wife and marry her soon."

"The jury believes she was a battered wife. They aren't going to buy something one of his mistresses says."

"We'll see, Jenna."

Chapter 41

"We are back on the record in The State of Oklahoma v. Claire Brown. I have received requested instructions from both sides. I have submitted my version and am here to hear any objections. State?"

"I object to the self-defense instruction, as well as the battered women's instruction. Further, I want an instruction that the Defendant has made inconsistent statements on the 911 call. She never claimed this abuse until well after the event."

"Save it, Ms. Miller. Ms. Steele, the law requires that I give the instruction if there is any evidence of self-defense, which the Defendant presented. I'm not sure what she said to 911 is inconsistent, rather incomplete, but you are welcome to argue that.

"Ms. Miller, I'll hear arguments from you."

"I would like the instruction about the evidence of deceased's character because I'm sure Ms. Steele is going to argue on that point. I may have missed it, but I didn't see the credibility of the Defendant as a witness or credibility of opinion witnesses' instructions."

"I'll allow those. Anything else, State?"

"What about the use of information relied upon by opinion witnesses?"

"I'll add that."

"Now, State over the lunch break, I received a request for lesser included instructions."

"Yes, Your Honor."

"Defendant?"

"The Defendant objects to those instructions."

"I'm including lesser included offense instructions. I believe that the evidence in the record could support first degree murder, second degree murder, or manslaughter. I think this is fair to all parties, and I don't think the lesser included offenses should be any kind of surprise to the Defendant. It also appears that we will be hearing from a rebuttal witness. As much as I wanted to get to closing arguments today, I think we will start there tomorrow. This will also provide parties with time to adjust their arguments if necessary. Let's bring the jury in."

"What does that mean?"

"It means the State is concerned about not being able to get a first-degree murder conviction and asked for the jury to possibly convict you of second-degree murder—meaning you didn't have intent—or manslaughter meaning you may have thought you had to kill him in self-defense but didn't. You probably heard about imperfect self-defense in the Menendez brothers' case. I wanted to go all or nothing, and that is still our strategy, but it means the State acknowledges weaknesses in their case."

"Why did the judge give them that chance?"

"Judge Henson is a law-and-order judge, he doesn't want to look like he would be helping a potential murderer go free. Don't worry."

After the jury came in, Judge Henson asked, "State, any rebuttal?"

Blake stood, "Yes, the State calls Rachael Collins."

"Miss, would you tell us how you knew the

deceased?"

"He and I began dating two years ago. He gave me a promise ring and said he would marry me when he could."

"Do you still have that ring?"

"Yes, I'm wearing it on my right hand now."

"Can you show it to the jury?"

She showed them a platinum, diamond encrusted band.

"Did the Defendant know about your affair?"

"I believe so. He was with me more and more often. He told me he asked her for a divorce."

"Objection; hearsay."

"Sustained."

"Do you have any proof of this affair or that he bought you this ring?"

"These are cards and letters he wrote me, but he also paid for my condo. I had to move after he died."

"Objection, Your Honor, if these are in fact letters from the deceased, they are still hearsay."

"They are not being offered for the truth, but for state of mind."

"Let me look at what you intend to introduce." Judge Henson reviewed and called the attorneys up to the bench. "I'm not going to allow hearsay, but I will allow you to have her read this letter he wrote her about telling the Defendant and how she reacted."

"Can I have a copy of these?"

"Yes, here you go Ms. Miller."

When she went back to her table, she showed these to Claire. "Did you know about her?"

"No, but like I said I sensed there was another mistress."

"Is this his handwriting?"

"I've never known him to write letters. Cards, flowers, gifts, e-mails, yes, but not letters. Let me look through."

"Ms. Collins, would you read this section?"

"Rach, I finally told her it was over. She was furious, but at the same time, not surprised. Just stick with me a little longer. Our relationship can't come out. We have to keep a low profile though. I'm still a married father."

"No further questions."

Jenna pounced, "Ms. Collins, how do you know that Mr. Brown was talking about his wife?"

"Who else would he be talking about?"

"Were you aware that he had another mistress up until about a month before he died?"

"What? No, he didn't."

"You didn't know he was also sleeping with his secretary?"

"No, he wouldn't do that to me. You're lying."

"So, you didn't know that she testified two days ago that she believed that my client killed her husband because she found out about their affair?"

"No."

"How long had this affair gone on?"

"About two years."

"Yet you knew he was married and had a daughter?"

"Yes, unhappily married."

"So, you had no problem committing adultery?"

"No, he told me he was going to divorce her and marry me."

"Isn't that what all married men say?"

"I don't know, but we were in love. He hadn't been happy with her in years."

"Did he ever introduce you to his daughter?"

"No, I just saw pictures and videos."

"So, you expect the jury to believe that he was about to make you stepmother to a daughter that you had never met?"

"He was probably afraid his daughter would tell her mom."

"But if he really wanted to divorce her, wouldn't that be good?"

"It might cost him more in a divorce."

"But you don't know that; you are just guessing."

"I don't know for sure, no."

"Were you aware that while he beat his wife, he also regularly bought her gifts and was still having relations with his wife?"

"I assume he had to keep up appearances."

"You didn't really know much about Mr. Brown, did you?"

"I knew him better than anyone."

"Yet you didn't know he had another mistress and still regularly had sex with his wife?

"Let me ask you this. Were you allowed to date other people?"

"I didn't want to be with anyone else."

"That wasn't my question, would he allow you to date anyone else?"

"No."

"He had a double standard for himself and you then?"

"I still don't believe you about all that."

"Did you ever approach my client and tell her that

you were sleeping with her husband or that you two were in love?"

"No, I don't think that would have gone over well."

"With her or with Mr. Brown?"

"Probably neither."

"Do you think he would have quit paying for your life if you told his wife about your affair?"

"Maybe."

"Did you ever see him angry?"

"Sometimes when he talked about his wife."

"Nothing further."

"Any redirect, State?"

"State rests."

"We are adjourned for the day. We will instruct and argue this case at 9:00 A.M. tomorrow. Be prepared to leave your cell phones in the car or with my bailiff tomorrow. You cannot have them in deliberations."

"Claire, are you ok?"

"I'm nervous, but I know you've had me this whole time. I just have to keep trusting and believing. I'll see you tomorrow."

"Try to sleep. I feel good. That doesn't mean anything necessarily, but I'll finish up my outline and notes for tomorrow."

Chapter 42

When Jenna and Jaxson walked into her house, Jaxson spun her around and kissed her. "What's that for?"

"Do I need a reason?"

"No."

"But since you asked, I've been wanting to kiss you since this morning, and you were a badass in court today."

"Thank you, babe."

"Did I finally merit an endearment?"

"Hush. You know how I feel about you. I'm going to change out of this suit. I'm a little hungry, but I need to work on my closing with those lesser included instructions and add in my notes from today."

"What would you like to eat, and I'll take care of it."

"Anything light is fine."

"I'm going to take Blitz on a quick walk and grab something and bring it back. Please keep doors locked and alarm on. I will be back shortly."

"I promise. Trial is almost over, so I doubt I would be in any danger now."

"You received another text a couple days ago."

"And nothing else since. I'm fine."

"Let's not tempt fate. If you need me or anything happens, you call me immediately."

She walked over to him and put her arms around his neck. "I'll be fine. I promise I won't go anywhere. I'm just going to be working. I know you'll take care of me, even if it's just a bad dream like last night." She gave him a quick kiss and returned to the couch.

She added, subtracted, and rearranged her closing argument outline. She loved defense closings because a lot of it is rebuttal, so always at the beginning of her closing she goes right after what the prosecution just said, then goes into her prepared material. The doorbell startled her. She looked down at her app and only saw flowers in the view of the camera, so she jumped up, turned off the alarm and opened the door. "You're too sweet, Jax. You didn't have to do that."

"Don't make a sound or this may accidentally go off."

She would have recognized that voice anywhere. She couldn't move, scream, or do anything because she was too stunned. *What is he doing out of the mental hospital? How does he know where I live? Is he planning to shoot me?*

"Good girl. I've been watching you for days waiting for your new beau to give you a minute to yourself."

"What are you doing here?" She stammered.

"It's time for you to pay for what you did to me. I warned you. You think you could just move on without me? We need to get out of here before that guy comes back. He seems to care about you. He'll realize that I'm doing him a big favor. You would have turned on him too." He grabbed her by the arm and pushed her forward. The gun dug into her back until she got into his car parked a few houses down.

"Get in." As soon as she was in, he buckled her in and handcuffed her right arm to the door. "That's so you don't think about trying to escape. Don't worry. I have my own surveillance on your house. It will be fun watching the boyfriend squirm when he realizes you aren't there."

They drove for what seemed like forever when he stopped at a cabin on a dirt road. "What are we doing here?"

"Not your time to talk yet. I'll gag you if I must, but it won't be as fun. The game is just beginning." He pushed her up against the wall and stuck his tongue down her throat. "You aren't as good of a kisser as I remember, or maybe you just spent all of your energy on your guy last night."

"What do you mean?"

"I watched you two last night. It was such a sweet sight. His comforting you after your nightmare and then staying and cuddling you. How many men have you been with? Seems like you made me wait until we got married."

"I actually still haven't been with anyone. I spent all my time going to law school after you went away. Are you jealous? You cut off all contact with me, remember?"

"You betrayed me."

"You shot an innocent person and needed help. Help that I thought you would get in the hospital, but clearly you didn't."

He backhanded her across the room, and her head hit the table and she blacked out. "See, look what you made me do already."

****

241

Jaxson and Blitz bounded up the sidewalk, and instantly knew something was wrong. The door stood wide open. "Jenna? Jenna. Jenna!" Her phone and purse were still there, and all her notes were spread out. He ran to her garage just to make sure, but her car was there. He dialed 911 immediately.

"911. What's the address to your emergency?"

"2054 N.W. 119th Street. My girlfriend's been kidnapped. Contact Detective Meyers. He's been working on this case. She's been being threatened and stalked."

"Sir, how long has she been missing?"

"Less than thirty minutes. I just left her for a little bit."

"Sir, we can't file a missing persons case on an adult unless they have been missing for twenty-four hours at least. Maybe she just left you."

"She didn't just leave me. The door is ajar. Her phone and purse are here. Call Detective Meyers."

He hung up and went to her alarm system and saw a doorbell video and saw a man with flowers ring the doorbell and then he saw her open the door and the gun. He couldn't see the man's face. *Oh no! I shouldn't have left her for a minute. This is all my fault.* His phone rang, and it was Detective Meyers. He filled him in. He paced and didn't even know what to do. *Pull yourself together. You were a cop. But where do I start? I have no idea who took her or where.*

He went to the neighbors and started asking questions and asking to see if any of them had cameras that caught anything. A neighbor a few doors down showed him a video of her and a guy walking to a car, but all he could tell was that it was a black four-door sedan, which wasn't much help at all. Police and crime scene units arrived shortly. Det. Meyers said he had people calling the prosecutors and going to interview Lara Brown.

"This is all my fault. The trial was supposed to be over tomorrow, so I thought it would be ok. I just left for a few minutes to grab food and walk the dog while she worked on her case. The door was locked and the alarm on. I promised I would keep her safe."

"Jaxson, you have to calm down. You couldn't have known. Why did she answer the door?"

"She saw flowers. She probably thought it was me. I was just a few minutes behind according to the surveillance. She could be anywhere."

"We are putting an APB out on her and what we can on the car, but I do have to tell you something. That ex she talked about. He is no longer in the state mental hospital. Do you think it's possible he's the one doing this?"

"After all this time? Why? Had you talked to him?"

"No, we had been trying to find him and couldn't.

"We figured he just didn't have anything in his name because he'd been away for so long."

"When did he get out?"

"About a year ago, but no one had seen him in about six months. This case of hers received media attention. It's possible he saw her on there and decided to come after her."

"Clearly, the mental hospital didn't help him. He tried to kill someone once before. He had a gun. He shouldn't even have one with his condition."

"He probably stopped taking his meds. You know most of them do."

"Damn it. I can't lose her. Not now."

"We'll do everything we can, and we all will pray that we will catch a break. I know you know what you're doing. See if there is anything you can find to think of a place he might have taken her. Maybe somewhere that was special to them."

"She didn't talk much about that. She's very private. She was just starting to open up to me, but I'll dig into it. Before I left, she said she knew I would take care of her. I screwed that up. We have to find her before it's too late."

Chapter 43

Jenna opened her eyes and touched the back of her head that was pounding. She felt a cut back there. When she pulled her hand back, she saw blood. *Where am I?* Then she remembered Erik's kidnapping her. "Erik? Can we talk about this?" *My nightmare is coming true.*

"Good, you're awake.

"We need to make a video for your new beau."

"What are you talking about?"

"You think you were going to just move on and start a new relationship with someone new? You're mine. I went to jail and a mental hospital for you. I had to save you from the neighbor. You can believe me or not, but he was obsessed with you. I spent nearly ten years locked away from society for you. You decided to move on."

"I spent years in mourning over you. You blamed me and wouldn't talk to me. You broke my heart. I cried for months and missed you terribly. I didn't do anything but work for years. I just met Jaxson earlier this year, and you can even ask him, I just started opening up to him. I shut him down several times."

"I know I've been watching, but I thought you would have understood my warning. If you had just chucked him to the side, we could have been together again and all would have been fine, but you betrayed me again."

"I didn't even know you were out. How did I betray you? You never contacted me."

"You should have known, my dear. Now, you're going to sing one of our songs to your precious boy toy as a way of saying goodbye. That is after he sees you making out with me and professing your undying love for me."

"And then what? You think people will stop looking for me? I'm in the middle of a publicized murder trial. I can't just disappear."

"They will put someone else on the case or call a mistrial or something. Not my problem, but you have to dump Jaxson Stone—what a pretentious name—and then you and I will start our life anew the way we were supposed to years ago."

"That's insane. I've barely played or sang since then. We've both changed in the last decade. We can't just up and move. My Aunt Rose has cancer. I can't leave her either."

"It's either you do as I say and leave and start over with me or you die. Take your pick." He rubbed the gun against the side of her head. He set up the camera and the music then. "You were such a lovely and talented actress. I've written you a script with staging and a song for you to perform, but before that. Let's tune in to your boy!" He showed her surveillance of her home.

"This is great. He's frantic running around. I think I may have even seen a tear. How sweet! He'll get a quick immersion into what loving you is really like."

"If I'm so bad, why are you so desperate to start over with me?"

He slapped her again. "Watch your mouth. You know chemistry like ours is once in a lifetime. Now.

Lights! Camera! Action!"

With her cheek stinging, she started the prepared statement. "Jax, I'm sorry but I need to reunite with my first love Erik. He and I belong together. We're leaving soon. Don't try to find me. I shouldn't have betrayed him. I knew he would come back for me. Bad things happen to people that love me, but he is willing to give me another chance. I'm sure your ex would take you back or you will find someone better than me for you. Have the public defender's office assign someone else to finish Claire's case. I'm sure they can get a continuance of a day or two ."

The strains of John Mayer's "Slow Dancing in a Burning Room" began to play. This was one of her and Erik's duets they did. The instinctual memory of how they would sing and dance to this song came back to her. She sang, "It's not a silly little moment. It's not the storm before the calm. This is the deep and dying breath of this love that we've been working on…"

Erik started singing and dancing with her as if they were on stage again. She was cringing inside but tried not to let it show because he seemed to have this whole thing planned. At the end of the song, Erik pulled her in and kissed her. It took everything in her not to vomit. He then looked directly at the camera and said, "Mr. Stone, she's mine again. If you really love her, you will stop searching for her and let her go with me or I might just kill her. She'll either be with me or with no one."

He started kissing her and pawing at her for the camera until he switched it off with the remote. Then, he sent the video to Jaxson.

****

When Jaxson's phone dinged, he immediately

opened the video and saw Jenna and called out for
Detective Meyers. He could see that her face was red
and swollen and saw blood on her shirt. "I told you this
guy was psychotic. We need to find her. Let's ping the
phone number or run a trace on where this video came
from."

"No luck. He encrypted the IP address well," said
one of the other officers.

"What about pinging the phone?"

"We have to get a warrant, and she may be with
him willingly.

"Have you lost your mind? There's blood on her
shirt, and could you not see that she was just trying to
appease him. Look, my family has money. Whatever it
costs. I just want her back in one piece. I'm not buying
that for a second. Forget about me, she's put months
into Claire's case. She wouldn't just take off and not
finish it."

"I'm working on it, Jaxson. You have to calm
down," Det. Meyers piped in. "The D.A. Investigator is
getting the warrant."

****

"Erik, I did what you asked. My head is killing me.
I may have a concussion. I need to see a doctor."

"Not falling for that. I have ibuprofen and will get
you an ice pack and will keep you awake. You need to
show me at least as much attention as you gave that
investigator." He came over and handcuffed her wrists
to the bed and undressed.

"Erik, no. If you want me to be with you, you've
got to give me time."

"You've had years. We were set to be married
within a month of when I got arrested. You loved me

then. Have you forgotten?"

"No, but you can't expect me to have sex with you after you kidnapped me at gunpoint and made me send that video to him?"

"I can. I've waited for years on you. I was waiting until we got married. Then, because of you I was locked up. I've been waiting to see you again. I'm not waiting anymore."

"Erik, please not like this. Please! I'll go with you, but not tonight. Not now." He ignored her, undid her shorts, and pulled them off. He ripped open her button-down shirt and just looked at her in her underwear. "You look better than I imagined. I think you're in better shape than we were in college." He rubbed his hand up and down her.

She shivered and recoiled, but being cuffed to the bed, she couldn't move far. "We can do this the easy way or the hard way; your choice, but you won't like the hard way. I met a lot of interesting people in jail and in the hospital. They told me lots of stories and taught me a lot. Don't test me." He then moved to the side and took pictures of her.

"Why are you doing that?"

"More stuff to send to your boyfriend so he'll get the hint if he hasn't yet."

"Erik, please don't. I don't want pictures of me like this out there."

"You aren't in charge, so shut up." He snapped more pictures, and she could tell he was sending them. "You're about to go live. I sent your boy a link, so he can watch this." He started to kiss her and was about to pin her down when she kneed him in the groin knocking him off her.

"You're going to pay for that!" He grabbed her ankle and jerked her, causing her to scream in pain as he tied her legs together, jerking her cuffed wrists away from the bed.

****

Jaxson was on the phone with Aunt Rosie. "Do you know where Jenna might keep pictures or mementos from her relationship with Erik? Did they have a special place where they went? Do you know about his family?"

Det. Meyers listened and hoped Jenna's aunt knew something, because Erik's parents were dead, and he had no siblings. They were looking for any properties that they might own, but so far hadn't found anything.

He went into her bedroom and found the boxes Rose told him about and realized how sentimental Jenna really was. She had every note, picture, program, mementos from their whole relationship. *Well, this is going to take a while. I just hope I find some clue as to where he took her.*

His text tone went off and he saw a link. When he opened it, he saw her tied to a bed and the man taking his clothes off and ripping hers off. "Damnit!"

"What's wrong?" Det. Meyers came in.

"Look at this monster, he's about to rape her. We've got to find a way to trace this live feed."

"She's fighting him."

"She's handcuffed. He's just going to hurt her more. I promised to protect her. I'll never be able to forgive myself if she gets hurt."

"You said that you would spend money. I know of a guy that's an expert hacker. He might be able to help, but he doesn't do good deeds."

"Call him now. Whatever he wants, I'll pay."

****

"Erik, what do you really want? To keep me as your prisoner? I don't really believe you want to kill me. At one time, you did love me. This isn't you. You were sweet and soulful. You're not this guy. How did you get here?"

He ignored her and kept pacing and looking through the blinds, so she started again. "When did you get released from the hospital? Are you taking your medication? Where have you been? What about your parents? They won't want to see you in trouble again."

"My parents are dead."

"Oh no. What happened?"

"Stop pretending like you care."

"Erik, you know I loved you, and part of me still does. What happened to your parents?"

He glared at her. "Mom killed herself about a year after I was put into the hospital. Dad had a heart attack a couple of years ago. Probably from the stress of my being locked up and Mom dying. It's all your fault."

"I'm so sorry. I know how close you were to your mom. She was a great woman."

"She was, and she loved you, yet you betrayed her too."

"Erik, I didn't know what else to do. I wanted you to get help. You weren't yourself anymore. It seems like you still aren't. I fell in love with you because you were so talented and devoted to your art. You had stopped caring about it. You had always been so loving, but you had become cold and distant those last few months. Much like you are now. You wouldn't talk to me anymore. After your arrest, you were a totally different person. I still loved you, but you shut me out. I wouldn't have left you, but you didn't give me a choice. It probably turned out for the best. I help people every day charged with crimes because of what happened with you."

"If you had really loved me, you would have helped me and not turned me into the police."

"They already had an idea and threatened to arrest me if I helped you."

"So, you chose yourself over me. About time you admitted it. I really did love you then. Nothing matters anymore. If you don't want to be with me in this life, you can be with me in the afterlife." He fingered the gun. "I can't believe you fell in love with someone else. I guess you never really loved me."

"That's not true, Erik. I did love you, and a part of me always will. I never expected to fall in love again, but I did. Ten years ago, I had to start over. I mourned you for years. You can't fault me for finally moving on. He's a good man."

"He's a trust fund baby. He's not your type. He doesn't even have to work. What do you know about that life?" She looked shocked because she had no idea. "You didn't know, did you? Guess he isn't perfect after all. Must not have wanted to share his money with you."

"You know I don't care about money."

"But he must, or he would have told you."

"Maybe he just wanted me to like him for him."

"Whatever. Go to sleep."

He put the gun in its holster at his waist and walked into another room. "Where are you going?"

"Don't worry about it."

****

"Have you figured anything out yet? This guy is clearly unstable. I'm scared to death for her."

"This guy is good, but I'm working on it. Your pacing back and forth behind me and asking me every couple of minutes isn't helping."

"Excuse me for being a pain, but this psycho may rape or kill my girlfriend."

"Jaxson, come here." Det. Meyers motioned him over. "Look, I know you're worried, but you're not helping. Go back and look through her mementos about her relationship with Erik. Maybe you'll find something in there."

Hours later, he hollered, "Meyers, come here. Does this look like the same place in the video?"

"Possibly, let's pull up that first video again."

"Look at that fireplace, it's the same."

"Does the picture say where this is?"

"Family reunion and two-year anniversary at Erik's grandparents."

"Finally, we have a lead!" Meyers and he both got to work on their databases. The computer guy finally said, "I've finally traced the IP address to a place in Guthrie."

"Is it this?" He showed him an address he found in his database.

"Yes."

He ran to his vehicle. Meyers nearly tackled him. "We've called Guthrie PD, and our guys are on the way. You aren't on the force anymore. You can't go."

"You can arrest me later, but no way I'm not going. She's been with that maniac for over twelve hours!"

"Fine, get in with me. You'll get pulled over going as fast as I know you'll drive."

Chapter 44

Jenna yawned and tried to stretch, but her body felt heavy, and her wrists were stinging. She looked around and realized she wasn't cuffed to the bed anymore. Erik was lying beside her with an arm over her chest. *Oh no! Please God, don't let him have had sex with me while I was sleeping.* She realized then that she was now wearing a dress. *Did he buy a dress for me to wear? This is weird.* She slowly tried to crawl out of bed. He didn't stir. *He always was such a sound sleeper. Maybe I can get out before he wakes up.*

She looked at the clock and realized it's 7 A.M. *I hope the Court has been notified and they continue this trial for a day or two. My head hurts so bad. Where are my shoes? This house is way out here, so if I manage to get out, I'm going to have to walk awhile. The concrete is way too hot to walk barefoot.* She looked around and saw his cell phone. She took it off the table and moved to the front of the house. She wanted to call Jaxson but, of course, he had a passcode. She could still make an emergency call though.

"911 what's the address to your emergency?"

"I don't know. This is Jenna Miller. I was kidnapped last night by my ex-boyfriend," she whispered.

"Ma'am, I can't understand you. You are going to have to speak up."

She inched to the front door and turned the handle, but nothing happened. She realized she needed a key to the deadbolt.

"Ma'am?"

"I'm still in the house. He's asleep, and I'm trying to whisper and find a way out. The front door requires a deadbolt key."

"What about a garage?"

"There isn't one. This is like a cabin. I'm trying to get to the backdoor." The floor squeaked echoing through the open room. *Please God, help me.* She tiptoed to the back door and saw it was just like the front door. "I can't get out. Please ping the phone or something. I'm sure he's going to wake up any second, and it will be worse when he realizes I called you."

She felt cold steel at the back of her neck. "Yes, it will. Now, give me the phone." She complied. "Thought you'd be able to get out before I woke up, huh? I tried to do a good deed and let you stay dressed and untied, and this is how you repay me. I even let you sleep and didn't have sex with you. I easily could have."

"I appreciate that; I really do, but I can't stay here. I have to get to court to finish this trial."

"You aren't in any shape to go to court. No, we will just have to move on quicker than I planned." He rubbed the gun up and down her chest. "Are you going to fight me again, or is this gun enough of a reason for you to behave?"

Goosebumps covered her arms. She was out of ideas. "Whatever you want, Erik. I don't want to die."

"That's better. Now, first thing, kiss me like you did that investigator this week."

Bile rose in her throat, and her heart fell. *Jaxson, forgive me.* She leaned forward, wrapped her arms around his neck and kissed him. He kissed her back wholeheartedly, but she still felt the gun in her back. He then picked her up and wrapped her legs around him.

"That's better, baby."

"Can you put the gun away now?"

"Not so fast."

What does that mean? I just hope police are on the way. He walked her outside and opened the trunk. "No, Erik, please don't put me in the trunk. You know I hate of not being able to move around. I can't handle that."

"You've left me no other choice." He injected her with something and threw her into the trunk.

She started screaming, kicking, and hitting, but it was no use. No one could hear her, and he threw her down in there and shut it before she could do anything. She searched the trunk for any kind of escape hatch, but nothing was working. Her breaths came quicker and shallower. She was hyperventilating now. She tried to calm herself, but it wasn't working. *God, please don't let me die in here.* Her limbs started to feel heavy. She couldn't keep her eyes open. Did he give her something? She fell unconscious then.

****

"Meyers. Yes, I'm working that case now. So, she's alive? We're on our way. I hope we're not too late."

"Who was that? What is it?"

"So, Jenna somehow got his phone and called 911, but couldn't get out of the house. The dispatcher said the last thing she heard before the line went dead was a man saying, 'Give me the phone.' "

"Hurry up. He could have shot her after that."

"If he wanted to kill her, he could have done that anytime last night. His plan isn't to kill her. He wants her with him."

"Did you not hear his ranting about her betraying him? She called the police, don't you get it?"

"Stone, shut up and let's just get there." His speedometer went over 100 mph then. When they arrived, two other officers were on scene and Erik was kneeling on the ground with his hands above his head.

He heard them asking, "Where is she?" Erik didn't move and didn't say a word. He ran from the car toward him. "What did you do to her?"

"I just saved you a lot of trouble, man. You should be thanking me."

He punched him in the face. Meyers pulled him off. "Take a walk before I do have to arrest you."

"Did you not just see him assault me? Why isn't he in cuffs?"

"I didn't see anything. Now, what have you done with Ms. Miller?" Erik just smiled at the officers.

The patrol officers came out of the house. "She's nowhere inside. We found a few spots of blood, but nothing to indicate that he killed her in there."

"Get a search warrant!" Meyers shouted at the other cops. "We need to search every inch of this property. Get the K-9s over here."

"No! This can't be happening. That son of a bitch knows where she's at. Give me a few minutes with him."

"Get him out of here!" Meyers shouted.

About thirty minutes later, a K-9 handler and his dog came out and started searching the grounds. The

German Shepherd was sniffing around and sat down behind the trunk of the vehicle. "We need to get this trunk open now," the handler called.

He sat and watched in horror. *Would she still be alive if she was in the trunk?* He prayed harder than he ever had as he ran over to the car. "She's alive. Unconscious, but alive."

"Thank God!" he yelled, ran back in past the police tape, grabbed her hand, and kissed her forehead. "Baby, please wake up, I'm so sorry."

"Are you coming in the ambulance?"

"Yes, I'm her boyfriend."

"Come on, but stay out of our way. She is stable. We are going to start an IV. It seems like maybe she was drugged with something."

He bowed his head and just kept praying that she would be ok.

Chapter 45

After Jenna was admitted into the ER, she slowly opened her eyes and saw Jaxson sitting by her bedside. "I'm sorry, Jax."

"Jenna! You're awake!" He rushed over to her and hugged and kissed her on top of the head. "What in the world are you sorry for?"

"I told you I would be fine and wouldn't open the door, but I thought it was you bringing flowers back because it seemed like something you would do."

"It is, and I did bring you a present back, but not flowers. Do you want it now?"

"If you still want to give it to me."

"I would give you anything in the world. I'm so sorry I left you at all. None of this would have happened."

"That is not true. Erik might have just shot you. He was furious about us being together. He saw it as a betrayal. I'm glad you weren't there."

He couldn't believe that she was worried about him. He pulled out the jewelry box and handed it to her. She opened it and gasped. "A diamond necklace! That's not a little gift."

"Do you like it?"

"It's beautiful. I love it. I can't wait to wear it, but it's too much."

"That's something we need to talk about."

"Don't worry, Erik told me you were a trust fund baby and that you didn't trust me. I told him, you probably just wanted to be liked for you and not for your money. I work at the public defender's office, I'm not all that concerned about money."

"I know you're not. I'm not either, which is why I still work, but I would spend all of it to make you happy." He bent down to kiss her gently. "I'm such a jerk. Let me get a nurse. I'm sure you're in pain."

"Sharp stabbing pains in the back of my head, but a little better than earlier. My cheek kinda hurts too. Oh no, what about Claire?"

"Judge Henson continued everything until Monday or until you're ready or could get someone else up to speed."

"I'm doing my closing. Have they checked to see if I have a concussion or if he broke my wrist?"

"They ran an MRI but haven't gotten the results back. He apparently gave you a shot of a sedative before he put you in the trunk."

"I was terrified I was going to die." She let the tears fall and held onto Jaxson.

Det. Meyers walked in. "So glad you are awake, Ms. Miller. I thought this boy here was going to have a nervous breakdown. By the way, Erik wants to press charges against you for breaking his nose. I don't know if the district attorney will pick up the charges, but a report was turned in."

"What? Are you serious?"

"Broke his nose, what did I miss?"

"He wouldn't tell us where you were. I got a little upset and may have punched him in the face."

"More like he made a running leap and threw his

entire bodyweight at him. I'm surprised he doesn't have more broken bones. He was quite difficult to pull off him. I'm just letting you know."

The doctor came in then. "Ms. Miller, you have a mild concussion, so we are going to keep you overnight for observation. Your wrist is badly sprained and swollen but not broken. I need to ask you several personal questions, do we need to clear the room?"

Det. Meyers left on his own. "No, this is my boyfriend. We can talk in front of him."

"I need to know if I need to have a nurse do a rape kit on you. You were passed out, and we knew there was concern over that."

"I don't think so. He didn't when I was awake anyway. I was worried about it this morning, but I really don't think he did. He said (she used air quotes) that he could have had sex with me, but he let me sleep."

"I think we should have a nurse do an exam just to be sure. We did find drugs in your system, and it's possible you don't remember or were too knocked out to know. I've prescribed you mild narcotics. Your nurse should be here to administer them soon."

She nodded. After he left, she grabbed Jaxson's hand again. "I'm sorry about that too."

"Jen, if you don't stop apologizing for stuff that is in no way your fault, I'm going to get mad."

"I don't know how much you saw or know, but I had to kiss him and touch him. Thankfully, he didn't rape me, or at least I don't think he did."

"You did what you had to do to survive, so don't ever mention it again. Though if he had gone much further on the video that I saw, I probably would have killed him."

"I knew you wouldn't give up. I just wanted to come home to you."

"Jen, I love you. Meyers was right. I was a complete mess. I couldn't lose you."

"I love you too." He leaned over and kissed her. "Wait, I need to call Rosie!"

"I called her, and she is on her way."

"So, am I going to have to represent you in Logan County?"

"I'm not too worried, but I'll call my dad. He's a lawyer in Tulsa. Don't worry about it. I'm not going anywhere, and if I have to sit in a jail for a bit once you're ok, I'd still do it again."

Chapter 46

"We are back on the record in The State of Oklahoma v. Claire Brown, outside the presence of the jury. We were set to begin closing arguments on Friday, but unfortunately some unexpected and abnormal things happened. Ms. Miller, are you okay to move forward this morning? I understand that you were in the hospital at least overnight this weekend."

"I am fine and ready to proceed. I rested over the weekend. I have talked to my client, and she is confident in my abilities and wants to finish up."

"State, any reservations about finishing today?"

"No, Your Honor, I think the people of this county and the jurors have waited long enough."

"Bring in the jury."

It took thirty minutes for Judge Henson to read all the instructions. She followed along for a lot of it, but she also reviewed her notes and outlines as well while he talked. As the adrenaline rushed through her, she felt her heart pounding through her chest. She kept her hands underneath the table so that she didn't drum her fingers on the table or touch her face.

Blake rose to do the prosecutor's first closing argument. She poised herself to write and combat what he said before she delivered the rest of her argument. "This is a simple case of a woman who married her first real boyfriend and became a young housewife and mother and sacrificed her college education and career for her husband. She signed a very restrictive pre-nup. She was miserable with her husband. Whether he was as bad as she claimed or not, she felt her only way out was to kill her husband. She admitted to knowing about his affairs. You heard from two different women who were having affairs with her late husband shortly before his death. She couldn't divorce him because she feared losing her daughter and the money, and if he divorced her, she would also lose out.

"The jury instructions tell you to use your common sense. The Defendant said nothing about being a battered wife until after she killed her husband. She didn't tell doctors. She didn't tell her mother. The Defense didn't put up one person who said that they saw the deceased abuse her at all. This expert that they had testify to try to rationalize and explain why she didn't tell anyone until he was dead, proved nothing. We aren't saying she isn't respected in her profession, but the Defense hired and paid for her. She specializes in working with victims of domestic violence, so she would likely be on the side of a female claiming abuse.

"As for Ms. Johnson, we know what her motivation was: money. She received $750,000 from the deceased and his family all those years ago. We know what she claimed, but would a true rape and assault victim take money rather than insisting that the predator went to prison? I submit to you that is where Ms. Brown got the idea. Use your common sense, spouses talk about their exes, and for her to claim that she didn't know the particulars just doesn't make sense.

"Let's talk about the jury instructions…"

She tuned out while he talked about the law, but his

main point was she stabbed him in the back, no defensive wounds on him or injuries on her, and that it was first degree murder. She knew that they were saving the big stuff for Mary Ann's final closing, so she got prepared. She rose as soon as she heard those magic words, "Return a verdict of guilty on murder in the first degree and sentence her to life in prison."

"Black widow or battered woman? Those seem to be your two choices in this trial. The prosecution would have you believe that she planned an elaborate murder plot to get out of an unhappy marriage with a sum of money. Let's use that common sense that the State told you to use. The deceased was twice my client's size. A former national champion football player who regularly worked out. Now, if you were going to plan to murder such a person, why would you do it with a butcher knife in the kitchen? What if he had seen her grab a knife and took it from her? What if you didn't stab him in the right place and he survived? She stayed home and made all his meals, why wouldn't she poison him? Or kill him in his sleep? Or any other ways that would have made more sense? Also, why do it in a messy and bloody way with your daughter at home? It doesn't make sense.

"The State says no one saw him abuse her. How many wifebeaters do you know that do it out in public so they can get arrested? What does that prove? Look at these pictures of all these injuries on her. Do you really think all these injuries were accidents? Including these broken ribs with a nice indention that looks surprisingly like his national championship ring. What about the isolation from her family and friends? The destruction of property in the house? The crack in the tile? Her destroyed mementos. Are there innocent explanations for all of that?

"You heard from his past serious girlfriend, and her testimony showed that the deceased had a *modus operandi* of controlling and abusing women when he was drunk and jealous and demanded sexual favors after abuse, particularly strangulation. In case the prosecutor tries to fool you, forcing sex—any kind on your wife or girlfriend after just beating her is rape. She couldn't consent. She wouldn't dare not to consent. He just showed her what he could do to her. She would go along with anything to make it stop.

"Remember hearing from the expert, that when in these situations, people either fight, flee, or freeze. We often hear about fight or flight, but the research shows that many people absolutely freeze. Afraid to fight. Afraid they can't outrun their attacker. Hollywood has shown us how many women that try to run and get caught in horror movies. That night she knew things were different, and she tried to escape only to be tackled onto the floor and then strangled to the point she couldn't breathe. At that moment, she knew it was fight or die. She thought about the one thing she loved more than her own life: her six-year-old daughter, Ashley, who would grow up without a mother if she didn't fight. So, she tried anything she could to get him to release the vise grip he had around her neck.

"She loved her husband. It may have been dysfunctional and unhealthy, but she loved him. That is why she stayed. She was codependent. She sacrificed everything about herself to be with him, but she loved her daughter more. She called 911 immediately and tried to stop the bleeding, but as the medical examiner told you, he died in seconds. The prosecutor may tell you it was a 'lucky shot' but there was nothing lucky about it. She has spent the last several months in jail. She hasn't been able to see her daughter. She had to relive and tell perfect strangers about intimate details of her marriage. She was already embarrassed and ashamed of her situation, but she had to tell a courtroom full of people.

"The State will likely argue to you that no one saw injuries on her that night. But let's look at the booking photo. It's not a great photo, but she has a swollen face and red eyes. Maybe nothing major, but she was clothed in this book-in photo. You wouldn't see red marks or bruises forming on her legs and back. You also wouldn't see marks on the back of her neck and under her hair. Remember she demonstrated how he was strangling her. You also can't see injuries to someone's head. No one looked for injuries from his dragging her by the hair. Common sense, ladies and gentlemen, no one checked her out medically. They don't know. The State has the burden; not us.

"The State has tried to make a major point out of the fact that my client didn't tell police that night, but that is absolutely her Constitutional right not to talk. And I can tell you, had she called me that night, I would have said never talk to the police, particularly at that point. You cannot hold that against her—no matter how much the State argues for that.

"Most importantly, please turn to your self-defense instructions, once we as the defense put on any evidence of self-defense, the State must prove that she did not act in self-defense beyond a reasonable doubt. They cannot and did not meet that burden. You heard testimony from my client. You heard witnesses that supported her life as a battered woman, from the education you received from the expert, from the deceased's ex-girlfriend who had a similar experience, and her mother who confirmed their deteriorating relationship. Even a few of the State's witnesses back up my client. The paramedic talked about symptoms of strangulation and frequent occurrences of domestic violence victims not seeking treatment. You heard from the medical examiner that the pictures of wounds introduced in this case most likely came from someone abusing her.

"She's not a black widow; she's a battered wife. The State didn't prove their black widow theory. They didn't disprove that she was a battered wife. Return a verdict of not guilty and send her home. Thank you!"

Mary Ann was at the podium before she even sat down. "What evidence of self-defense? The Defendant's self-serving testimony? Pictures of bruises or marks taken out of context? Injuries when she sought medical treatment and didn't say she wasn't abused. So, either she lied at the hospital or on the stand. Let's give her the benefit of the doubt, he was possessive and controlling and made her drop out and stay home, that doesn't deserve the death penalty. This isn't the 1970s or 80s when no domestic violence shelters existed, and marital rape wasn't a crime. We have been in the middle of the #metoo movement now for years. If she were a victim, she would have been welcomed with open arms and helped and protected, but she didn't seek help, she stabbed her husband in the back.

"A man in his early thirties with a young daughter, a career that was skyrocketing, and a whole life ahead of him. She claimed to love their daughter, and that was who she was thinking about when she stabbed him, but didn't she deserve to grow up with a father? The Defendant even testified that he was a great father and doted on their child. This nonsense that she couldn't get a lawyer to help her because he controlled the money is just that—nonsense. You can apply for legal aid attorneys and for the court to order the other side to pay your fees. If attorneys know there is marital money, they may even take it and sue for attorney fees in the process. She had options. She could have left while he was at work. She could have called the police after an alleged beating while he was gone. She could have filed for a protective order. She could have contacted her family to help her.

"She could have gotten a divorce and child support if she was so unhappy or he was such a monster, but instead, she stabbed him in the back with her daughter in the house. It's just a miracle that the daughter didn't wake up and see this. You might think I have no sympathy for domestic violence victims, but that isn't true. I have a lot of sympathy for real victims, but when women like the Defendant claim to be a victim of domestic violence and sexual assault when they aren't, they make it that much harder for true victims to get justice. Don't fall for it!

"As defense counsel said, the deceased was much larger than the Defendant; do you think she would have been able to grab a knife and stab him in the back without his realizing she grabbed a knife and taking it away from her? Could she really have even reached around him if he were really strangling her? I don't think so. So what if she had red eyes? What does that prove? Maybe she was crying after she realized what she did? We don't know. No, she had to stab him in the back when he didn't see it coming. That was planned. She intended to kill him. She wanted their daughter, the house, and all the money for herself. She wanted to start over, and the only way she saw to do that was to get rid of him. I would submit she is exactly a black widow. When he had served his purpose, she murdered him with the plan of moving on. This was intentional. She was come over by a heat of passion. She wasn't just trying to hurt him or get him off her. She grabbed a butcher knife and stabbed him in the back of his heart; what a double meaning there. Ladies and gentlemen, that's first-degree murder. Return a verdict of guilty and send her to prison for the rest of her life. Thank you."

The jury walked out then to start their deliberations.

"Thank you for believing in me and fighting for me!" Claire hugged her then.

"I told you I would. I hope it's enough. I need to walk around. I hate the waiting. I'll be nearby."

Chapter 47

Jenna and Jaxson were walking hand-in-hand across the street to get a sandwich and a drink. "How are you feeling? I thought you were amazing."

"Thanks, babe. I feel like they should be with me, but honestly, I don't know. I hate the waiting."

"Would you still like to take a little vacation when this is over?"

"Absolutely. Where are we going?"

"Where would you like to go?"

"I don't know. I never go anywhere because I work all the time. Are they going to file charges on you?"

"No, my dad got the bond dropped to OR and talked to the district attorney. He said that he would have done the same thing. I want you to meet my parents soon too."

"They probably won't like me given what they are first hearing about me." Her phone started ringing. "That's Judge Henson's chambers. It's not even been thirty minutes. Could they already have a not guilty verdict? I wouldn't think they could have voted to convict and settle on punishment already?"

"Hello?"

"Jenna, the jury has a question, so I need you to come back."

"On my way, Judge."

****

She walked in and saw Mary Ann already waiting. "I think it's pretty typical in that I say you have all of the information you decide in your instructions." Judge handed her the written question. "Do we have to all agree on first degree murder before we look at other lesser included offenses?"

"State, what do you think?"

"I agree."

"Defendant?"

"Yes."

She walked back into the courtroom and told Claire about the question. "Oh no! That must mean they are talking about convicting me. Even if convicted of manslaughter, I'll lose Ashley."

"Stay calm. You never know what all is going on in their heads, so try not to panic."

She walked back out to Jaxson and filled him in. "I don't like this at all. I don't want to sit here or answer questions from the office. Can we go down to the car?"

"Whatever you want." As they got on the elevator, he asked, "What about New York?"

"What about it?"

"For a vacation. I'm sure you're dying to see a Broadway show."

"That's a little more expensive than what I was thinking."

"What did I tell you about money?"

"I'm not sure I will get used to that."

When they were sitting in his BMW, her breathing became shallow, and she drummed her fingers on the doorframe. "I'm worried. I thought I had the jury, but maybe my head is still scrambled. She is counting on me."

"Hey, you did absolutely everything you could, and it may still be fine. In fact, I really think that it will."

"We may be waiting for hours I'm going to push back the seat and maybe take a little nap. I'm so tired."

About an hour later, she woke up. "How bad does my hair look?"

"You look beautiful as always, why?"

"I think we should go sit up there with Claire. She has to be way more anxious than me."

****

"This is taking a long time. Is that good or bad?" Claire asked, biting her lip.

"Hard to say, but it hasn't even been three hours, and on a murder case that isn't long. They also ordered and had lunch for about an hour of that time. They also had to get settled, use the bathroom, and pick a foreman. It's early in the day. If it's later in the day, they tend to come back quicker. Try to stay calm."

Just then a bell sounded. Judge Henson walked out then. "We have a verdict. All rise for the jury to enter." The courtroom was packed with other attorneys from the district attorney's office and public defender's office, family on both sides, and media waiting to hear the verdict. "Before they get here, I would caution everyone not to react regardless of the outcome. Please stand for the jury."

"Welcome back, ladies and gentlemen. Have you selected a foreperson?"

A woman on the back row stood and announced, "Yes, Your Honor."

"Have you reached a unanimous verdict?"

"Yes."

"My bailiff will pick up the verdict form from

you."

The judge looked at the form and handed it to the Court Clerk. "Defendant, please rise for the reading of the verdict."

Jenna didn't let go of Claire's hand, though her breath caught in her throat. She could feel the blood pulsing through her. "The State of Oklahoma versus Claire Brown Verdict Form-Murder in the First Degree. We the jury empaneled and sworn find the Defendant Not Guilty."

She squeezed her hand as tightly as she could to keep her from saying anything. Claire burst into tears. She heard whispered "oohs" were heard throughout the courtroom despite the admonishment.

"Quiet. Thank you for your service. You are free to go. Everyone but the jury is to remain in the courtroom until they have exited. We couldn't have these trials without your service. It is totally up to you as to whether you answer questions about your service. If anyone harasses you or criticizes your service, you contact my office."

Claire turned and grabbed onto her. "Thank you. Thank you so much!" Tears streamed down her face.

"You're welcome. Sometimes our system works out." She fell back into her chair and raised her head to heaven and whispered, "Thank you, Lord."

Lara stalked over to Claire. "Don't think that this is over. I'll sue you and keep you in court for years before you see a dime of our money. You won't get Ashley either."

"Ma'am, you need to back up." Jenna stepped in front of her, and Lara slapped her. "Bitch, how dare you!"

Jaxson jumped over the well, but the courtroom deputy already stepped in and pulled her back. "Ms. Miller, do you want to press charges?"

"No, just get her out of here."

"I told you she was crazy."

"You won today, Claire. I don't typically do custody stuff, but I'll use a little personal time, and we will file an emergency application to get your daughter back tomorrow. They will have to book you out at the jail."

Claire's mom and sister were enveloping them both in a hug. "When can I get her out of the jail?" Khara asked the guard.

"We will start booking her out as soon as we get back. It shouldn't be too long, but we need to get going."

Chapter 48

Judge White signed a writ for the immediate return of Ashley to Claire on the condition that she engage in domestic violence and family counseling with the child. The deputies picked her up from Lara. Claire was waiting at her house for them to arrive with Ashley. When the doorbell rang, she jumped a little bit, but as soon as Jaxson opened the door, a beautiful blonde girl ran straight into her mom's arms.

"Momma, I missed you so much."

"We'll give you all a few minutes." Jaxson went outside and talked with the deputies for a minute, and she went into her room and silently said a prayer thanking God that everything worked out ok.

As she started to walk back out into her living room she heard, "I did what you said, Momma, and didn't tell anyone what happened. I told my counselor that Daddy was mean to you because I keep having nightmares, but nothing else. I was so worried about you."

Jenna froze in her tracks and gasped. "What really happened? I guess you played me for a fool."

"It's not like that." Claire gestured with her palms up.

Jenna shook her head again. "I thought you were being all noble by protecting your daughter, but she wasn't asleep. You can't be charged again, so you might as well tell me."

"Everything I tell you is still privileged, right?" Claire asked.

Jenna nodded and whispered, "Yes."

Claire explained, "I didn't stab Devon. The prosecutor was right. I couldn't get my arms out from under him. He had me pinned all the way down."

Jenna narrowed her eyes. "Then, who did?"

"The only person in the world I would go to prison for."

She clasped her hands over her head. "What? No. She's just a child. She couldn't have done it."

"She had to grow up a lot sooner than most. She saw a lot of the fights. He caught her a couple times and that would end up being my fault too. When he slammed me onto the kitchen island, silverware and pans went flying. I really thought I was going to die. That was all true. Suddenly, he let go and fell forward, and I saw her standing behind him, and I knew what happened. I screamed at her to go back to bed and pretend she didn't know anything. It was my fault. I wasn't going to let her be locked away for something I should have stopped."

"You realize that you committed perjury on the stand, don't you?"

Claire's posture changed. She stood tall and crossed her arms behind her back. "Only two people know that: you and my daughter, but I was careful with how I testified that I must have stabbed him in my struggle."

Ashley shrieked, "He was hurting my mom. I had to stop him."

Jenna's eyes were wide as she looked at the two

women and put her head in her hands, trying to absorb what she just heard.

Claire answered, "Everything else I told you was true. Just not who did the stabbing. He was a bad man."

Jenna looked up. "I guess he won't hurt anyone else. I think y'all need to leave now."

"We appreciate everything you did for us."

The girl's eyes looked vacant and pleased. Goosebumps covered Jenna's arms. She wondered about that little girl. *Was she a sociopath like her father, or did she just do what she had to do? Are killers born or made? Does everyone lie? Do we really know anyone?* Her eyes locked with Jaxson's as he came back in the house, and she again dreaded those legal ethics that prevented her from talking to him about it. "I'm not sure how much longer I can keep doing this."

A word about the author…

Shelley L. Levisay is an attorney, author, and piano teacher living in Shawnee, Oklahoma. She has a dog named Mayhem, who is a registered therapy dog and competes in nosework and weight pull competitions. She has two cats named Phantom and Shadow and two ferrets named Buster and Shelby. She is a classical pianist and soprano who sings in several choirs, outside of COVID times. Other than music, she spends her time reading books and listening to podcasts.

http://oklawandpopcultute.com

CPSIA information can be obtained
at www.ICGtesting.com
Printed in the USA
LVHW051510150623
749660LV00010B/807